The Silent Sister
The Diary of Margot Frank

Mazal Alouf-Mizrahi

authorHOUSE

AuthorHouse™
1663 Liberty Drive
Bloomington, IN 47403
www.authorhouse.com
Phone: 1-800-839-8640

© 2011 Mazal Alouf-Mizrahi. All rights reserved.

No part of this book may be reproduced, stored in a retrieval system, or transmitted by any means without the written permission of the author.

First published by AuthorHouse   2/18/2011

ISBN: 978-1-4567-2615-7 (e)
ISBN: 978-1-4567-2616-4 (hc)
ISBN: 978-1-4567-2617-1 (sc)

Library of Congress Control Number: 2011900270

Printed in the United States of America

Any people depicted in stock imagery provided by Thinkstock are models, and such images are being used for illustrative purposes only. Certain stock imagery © Thinkstock.

This book is printed on acid-free paper.

Because of the dynamic nature of the Internet, any Web addresses or links contained in this book may have changed since publication and may no longer be valid. The views expressed in this work are solely those of the author and do not necessarily reflect the views of the publisher, and the publisher hereby disclaims any responsibility for them.

This book is dedicated to the silenced voices of
Those who perished in the Holocaust—
Their voices echo in our memory.

Foreword

For several reasons it gives me great pleasure to write a foreword to this book.

I am deeply touched by the fact that the author, a young person whose own background is far removed from the experience of the Holocaust, should conceive of such a remarkable idea as to reconstruct the lost diary of a Jewish girl, who, one among millions, did not survive the horrors of the Shoah. To do that means to enter the victim's soul and relive her inner life to the bitter end. To accomplish that, one needs incredible sensitivity, imagination and talent, and the author seems to possess it all.

The amount of research carried out by the author that gives genuine authenticity to the life and times of the characters in the work, I also found very impressive.

After all these years, as a survivor of Auschwitz and Dachau, I still bear the pain of having lived while others did not. To contribute, even minimally, to sharing the memory of those who did not, helps ease the pain.

Thirty-eight years ago I was in Bergen-Belsen, searching for the grave of my father who perished there thirty-three years previously. Endlessly traversing the former camp site, now a vast open area studded by enormous mounds – mass graves – I did not find my father's grave, I did not find any traces of my father in this infinite graveyard. Except one immense mound, marked: "Here Lie 25,000 Bodies Killed in April 1945." I had been told my father was killed shortly before the camp's liberation, in April 1945. So this was it – his last resting place.

However, I found traces of Margot and Anne Frank. In a small museum on the camp site there hung Margot and Anne Frank's picture with captions detailing their last days and the dates of their deaths. One of these numerous mass graves was the last resting place of these two vibrant teens – vivacious Anne and her thoughtful, sensitive older sister, Margot.

I believe the reader will share my profound appreciation for the masterly reconstruction of Margot's diary that so vividly recaptures their lives and Margot's unfulfilled dreams.

Prof. Livia Bitton-Jackson
H.H. Lehman College
C.U.N.Y.

Preface

Margot Frank died in Bergen-Belsen, a concentration camp located in Germany proper, sometime in March 1945. She was nineteen. Her sister, Anne Frank, followed Margot in death later that month. The sisters died without family members to mourn their passing.

Anne Frank's diary, first published in Amsterdam and later translated into many different languages, became a symbol of the Holocaust or the Shoah, *the Hebrew word for "calamity." Those who read her diary or see the film adaptation of her personal trials and triumphs are moved by the tragic loss of such an innocent and radiant spirit. Anne's maturity and integrity shine through the pages. One reads the last lines of her diary with the feeling that he or she knew this young woman intimately, as a friend, a sister, or as a daughter—and grieves her tragic passing.*

Anne became the exemplar of the unfathomable loss of human potential, multiplied by six million. When her father, Otto, decided to go into hiding, Anne Frank took her diary along. Margot, her older sister by three years, did the same. Anne tells Kitty that she and Margot read each other's diary while in hiding (Friday, 16 October, 1942). However, Margot's diary was never found.

Indeed, we know very little about Margot. She was quite intelligent and modest; she was soft-spoken and refined. According to Anne she was the "prettiest, sweetest, most beautiful girl in the world." She wanted to move to Palestine, and she dreamed of becoming a nurse. She did not confide a great deal in people, aside for her mother, Edith, her father, and Anne. Miep Gies, who was on close terms with Anne, noted that Margot kept to herself.

Margot is the silent sister. On a deep level she represents the Holocaust and its atrocities just as much as Anne. One can even say that Margot represents the victims in a way that Anne does not—the silence that reverberates from the mass graves and from the strewn ashes of millions of babies, grandmothers, handicapped adults, teenagers, fathers, daughters and sons—all forever muted by the hatred and cruelty of "ordinary" fathers and sons—is the very silent voice of Margot herself.

Monumental loss of human life stains the annals of history. This short work aspires to lend a voice to one human life—a minute and infinitesimal sound—so that the cacophony of inhumanity may be illuminated by a spark of hope.

Mazal Alouf-Mizrahi

Margot Frank's Diary—*please* do not read.

April 1942

"No one can make you feel inferior without your consent." Eleanor Roosevelt believed this to be true. In fact, those are her very words. However I try, though, I find too many forces pulling me into the abyss of piercing inferiority. I was raised to be proud. I was raised to be secure. I am gifted. I am loved and cherished by all who know me, but I am miserable. I am a Jew in Nazi-occupied Amsterdam.

I do not consent to the collective abuse spewed on us each day. I do not consent to the laws forbidding taking a tram or riding a bicycle. I do not consent to the hated insignia I don each day, but my consent was never sought. *No one* is asked. We are commanded, and we obey. Such nonsense! Behaving like automatons goes against the very fabric of our identity as humans and as Jews. We inquire and we ponder. That is part of our essence. That is the Jew: hundreds of opinions, arguments, suggestions and solutions. It is a never-ending cycle.

I have kept diaries before. When I was eight or ten-years-old. I have not written in any journal since. I must be able to write—for I am not in the habit of speaking too much.

Right now I am too tired to write any more. It's a cool evening, and I've stayed up late four nights in a row…

I can't believe my first diary entry is such a dismal one.

***

Mrs. Bieber recommended writing in a diary to "help you feel connected when you feel most disconnected." I found this advice compelling, since I have, as of late, been feeling depressed and lonely. I don't sleep very well at night, not since the Queen capitulated to the Nazis in May. May 14, 1940. I wish I could forget that date. I remember Mummy frantic, calling her friends in Rotterdam, begging them to flee the city days before the terrible bombardment by the German air force, the Luftwaffe—God curse them! Since then I have been breathing a heavy mist. My nails are terribly gnawed at; sometimes my fingers hurt when I write. My cuticles are bleeding too. But my nails are the only testament to my distress. Otherwise, I hide my pain and fear behind a courteous demeanor and cheerful disposition.

I play ping-pong at least once a week to focus on a ball instead of distressing reports of rape and mass shootings. Jewish properties are being seized in my birth-town (Frankfurt-am-Main, as far as we know, is *Judenrein*) by Germans who have never earned their way into prosperity but who, for years, have ogled those who have. They send their sons to fight a battle for glory, for their *Furher*, who promises them more than the Lord promised the Hebrews upon their arrival in the Holy Land. But instead of giving his Germans all the honey and milk from flowing springs of bounty, Hitler simply dispossessed the Jews and handed over their belongings to the peasant farmers next door. Such treachery!

But this is the *best* of the news we've heard lately. There are rumors of concentration camps, mass ghettoes, roundups, nightmarish conditions, imprisonments, and worst of all, missing persons. The Jew is the main problem for the occupiers. They defile themselves with the very thought of the JEW. I am saddened to have Germans on Dutch soil; the Dutch don't deserve such inglorious occupation.

The Germans don't seem to understand why the Dutch are not more welcoming. They, after all, consider the Dutch *herrenvolk*, descendants of the same Aryan nation as Himmler and the other Nazi generals infamously photographed in the center of town. This past February the Dutch 'volk' reacted to the deportation of Jews to Mauthausen and various other anti-Jewish regulations with a strike. I heard other Europeans reacted with silence— this constitutes agreement as far as I am concerned. Anyway, the leaders of the strike were executed, and the Dutch, demoralized, walked away with shoulders slumped, defeated. Nearly the entire town joined forces and gathered in the city center that February morning. People who thought they were headed to work joined the strike out of solidarity. Many pinned the Queen's emblem on their lapels. Some held orange carnations, the prince's very favorite.

Anne and I stood on our balcony to see the drove of people marching toward the center. Excited, we thought that if people got together and protested, then perhaps the Germans would capitulate, or at least amend their policies. That was not to be. That terrible Arthur Seyss Inquart, the 'German civilian governor,' quickly eroded the stamina and morale of the Dutch by initiating arrests and penalties. Himmler himself authorized the deportation of one thousand protestors. On the second day Anne and I heard gun shots. Anne nearly lost control of her bowels; she was so frightened! We ran into our rooms and locked the doors. Mummy called from a shop and exhorted us to remain indoors. Anne started to cry. "I want Papa! I want Papa!" Since Papa was in the office (he did not join the strikers!), I phoned him there, and he was able to calm her down.

A proud and upright people by far, the Dutch endeavored to resist the anti-Jewish laws, the oppression, abuse, and the arrests. Senator Boehmcker's harsh measures cooled the hot passion of defiance. He is known to be both cruel and heartless. The Dutch feared any bloodshed; they also began to fear for their lives! And, of course! They resisted arrest. (Rumors of torture were hard to ignore, even by the most courageous.) They did not continue the strike. And that was the end of overt defiance. It has since become obvious to us all that the Germans intend to impose the Third Reich on Holland's citizens and The Hague. The Orange Rule is now overrun by Black thugs, the Nazi policemen. Even the Queen has a hard time masking her disgust for the occupiers. She speaks to the nation with great resolve and courage every evening. Many draw inspiration from her words. The radio is indispensible in that regard. We also listen to the BBC, but secretly and very quietly. I listen to her *all* the time.

It saddened me to learn that even the best of all intentions to preserve the rights of fellow citizens (Jews) were steamrollered by the Nazi machine. Who can prevail in the face of such wickedness, when the forces of evil's tools of destruction are more powerful than our feeble hopes for peace?

The only good thing that came from all this, I now realize, is that I feel more loved by Mummy and Daddy. Worst of all, of course, is the fear of the German policemen, deportation, arrest, terrible maltreatment for 'misdemeanors' and sleepless nights. The food rationing is not too bad, since Mummy has planted her own vegetable garden. We make do. We go to the theatre more than usual, and we enjoy sitting together in the evening, looking through travel brochures. (I decided I should tour Australia before I visit Kenya.) I don't know how much success we've had. Escaping our day-to-day lives is mostly temporary. Peace of mind is short-lived. I have little to complain about since I am in school most of the day, like most girls my age. All I know is that writing in this diary is the only respite I have from biting my nails, since I am busy using my fingers to write.

***

(I decided not to focus too much on days and dates since this journal or diary is more about my thoughts. Thoughts don't have a place in time. They simply exist in a cloud of present-ness. Anyway, I like to read previous entries and take note of the myriad thought-processes and emotions.)

Anne and I went to school as usual today. I rode my bike, to save time, and Anne walked with one of her many suitors. There is a law forbidding bike riding for Jews, but I do so in spite of it all. I simply fold my lapel over or cover the Star of David with my scarf. I cannot forgo one of my very few pleasures. The swiftness, the cool breeze, the energizing sensation I feel afterwards... (It's finally April. Why should I not enjoy the breeze?) I patiently rode past the front landscape to the side entrance where all the students used to neatly park their bikes. Today there were two bikes. Yesterday there were more. Most students handed over their bikes to the Nazis. We did too, but Father decided to keep one bicycle in case of an emergency. I ride it sometimes. One cannot deny, however, the very palpable fear of getting caught. Hence the small number of bikes. I glanced at my watch and realized I was a bit early. Instead of walking through the side entrance, I walked back to the front façade. I pushed at the heavy doors but felt someone on the other side pull at the same time. All of a sudden, my glasses dropped to the floor (the lenses fell out but were unbroken). I smelled a faint sulfur-like odor combined with stale coffee and heard a bellow, "Ach! Watch where you are going!" The man then muttered a curse in German (Jewish bitch). I was now truly unable to see, and all I could think was, 'It's too bad I can't smell instead!' The man with the most *terrible* breath I ever had the misfortune to breathe pushed past me and tried to pat himself, as if he were cleaning dust or dirt off his sleeve, with a hysterical obsessive beat. Pat! Pat! Pat!

I held the broken lenses carefully near my eyes to make sure I wouldn't forget this terribly ugly man, just in case I were ever to see him again. His left nostril boasted a mole, and his hair was combed neatly to the left, revealing elf-like ears. My heart skipped a beat when I took note of the Nazi insignia on his arm band. I kept on imagining meeting him again… if I did, I thought, I wouldn't say anything uncouth to him, but I would make sure to *think* of something rotten (like scoundrel and putrid murderer), and maybe I would even grimace. (I read somewhere that people can sense your thoughts.) I know he was trying to 'clean' himself because he believes I am 'vermin'. I then thought to myself that he could definitely start with his mouth. And if he is a Nazi, which he most probably is, his mind too.

I tried to fix my glasses in the corner of the school's foyer. Before I could succeed, a man approached me and asked if I was a student in the upper division. After I nodded, he handed me a grey sheet of paper and insisted that I fill in all of my personal information. He told me to make sure my identity card was not missing, since policemen will seek to identify me wherever I go—the theatre, the ferry, and so on. He was impatient. I was intimidated a bit and hurried as well. I placed one of the lenses on my cheekbone and winced to keep it in place. I quickly jotted our address… and I don't know why, but as I was writing down the information all I could do was stare at the reflection of the man's nostrils on the tip of his black and very, very shiny boots.

(His nose can best be described as "aquiline.") As I methodically wrote I felt a stone hit my heart. And I thought, for a very short second, 'Should I be doing this?' But the side of me that listens and respects others quickly silenced this voice, and I handed the piece of paper to the man, whom I then noticed was wearing a military cap. He had a very cold blue-eye stare. I felt violated and looked down at my own shoes. They were brown, in the oxford style, and not very pretty. Anne makes fun of them and calls them my "boy-shoes." By the time I regained my sense of self, the man's back was in front of my very non-Aryan face, and I felt I did something wrong, for once, for following instructions and respecting my elders.

The officer spoke in German, and he didn't know that I understood him. He asked the secretary in the lobby if the Jewish students were permitted to 'fraternize' with the kids from the Dutch public school. The secretary quickly answered 'No'! I couldn't help but think she was such a liar, since her daughter was known to be in *constant* contact with her boyfriend Jan, a non-Jew, a very handsome soccer player from the Dutch public school! But I would have done the same thing if I were in her shoes.

I rushed home after school—up until then I had left my identity card by my bedside (together with baby pictures of Anne and some summer photographs of Hanneli and baby Gaby). I rummaged through old papers and candy wrappers. There it was—my identity card.

My goodness! What a picture! I don't think I look that much better now, come to think of it….

Mummy said I don't need to worry, and Papa looked only mildly concerned. He then brushed it off and said that where we live now won't really matter. I found his response quite strange, but I did not pursue the matter.

***

Hello Silberg, one of Anne's friends, was detained by an officer today by *Oasis*. I think the policeman was trying to make an example of him. Thankfully, he had the identity card with him. Hello feigned bravery, but it was obvious from his knotted brows that he was quite nervous and agitated. Anne walked in after the episode. That was probably for the best, since she wouldn't have taken it too well…

Now I have to be extra careful with my bicycle.

***

I wrote a poem, an "Ode for my Bicycle."
As I ride my bicycle—
I am
a free butterfly dancing
in the luscious and abundant
green, red, orange field.
A nightingale sailing

the fiery wind
on a hot May afternoon.
A delicate lark singing its song
of everlasting bloom—
For my appendage wheels
are my wings—
flying
above, Beyond
countless stars;
Soaring freely
aimlessly
Without restraint.

No fear do I feel
No bondage
No shackles nor chains;

I, flying above horizons
Unknown,
Undiscovered landscapes of yore
I, the Sparrow of Freedom,
Am free to roam.

***

How I hate it when Henriette makes a fool out of me!

I overheard Henriette Hullender speaking to Aleida Rosenberg in the girls' bathroom during my break from laboratory practices. I don't know how they didn't realize someone else was in the bathroom; my legs were clearly visible underneath the stall door. As it happens, they were making fun of Professor Kahn, whom they believe is a "doofus" and a "freak." They imitated his "snorting" laugh and the constant whistling his buck teeth inevitably produce each time he says "fluorine" or "physics." They especially laughed when Aleida mimicked "phosphorous." I didn't enjoy hearing them make fun of Professor Kahn. I think he's a very nice man. Perhaps I would have forgiven them if it were not for the mention of "poor Mrs.

Kahn." I don't think that's within the bounds of poking fun at teachers, which is in many ways inevitable in a high-school setting. I flushed the toilet, making my presence obvious. Henriette managed a smirk, and Aleida applied some water to her unruly hair. She then tweezed her brows, which were pencil thin to begin with. Henriette glanced at herself and quickly applied some kohl to line her eyes. I wanted to let them know what I thought, but I didn't say anything. Henriette glanced at me, cocked her head and said, "Margot, you know, you really *do* have such a pretty face, but you look terribly awful in those glasses of yours." Aleida quipped, "Aren't they similar to Professor Kahn's?" Both girls giggled. I washed my hands and promptly left the lavatory. This was not the first instance either one was particularly 'helpful' or 'friendly.' I'm accustomed to their snobby ways; I just wish I didn't feel hurt. And I wish I had retaliated with a strong response to shut them up—for good!

***

New brassieres!

I had to be measured, *again*. Mother and I went to Fantasy Lingerie to buy a brassiere. We hurried along the street, afraid to stay out after dark. Anne insisted on coming along. Truth be told, I wanted to shop only with Mummy, but I thought perhaps Anne might feel left out…Lately, my brassieres have been too tight, and I noticed a sharp pain each time I raised my hand in class. Mother says I take after my namesake. (I assume that means she also had a 'healthy sized bosom.') I'm not so sure I am entirely satisfied with my 'chest-size-inheritance,' but alas it matters very little! I am a bit self-conscious about my breasts since there are nineteen boys in my class and *six* girls, and I catch the boys staring at my chest all the time! Jacques usually gawks at Henriette (all the boys do). But when she is not in class the ratio is down to 5/19, and I inevitably become the object of his stares. For that reason I asked the saleswoman if she had a "special brassiere to minimize the chest," as I aptly put it. She laughed. And then she asked, "Why would you want *that*?" Most of her customers inserted cups into their brassieres…I didn't want to explain to her my specific concerns, so I settled for a regular bra in a larger cup size, to my disappointment. I guess I'll wear larger-sized shirts instead.

The Silent Sister

I am not self-conscious when I am all alone, but sometimes I *do* stare at my chest and wonder when my breasts became this way…

I'll never forget the first time Mummy bought me a brassiere. I hated wearing it!

I felt barricaded in my own clothes. I resented the brassiere at first. Pink ones with bows did little to assuage my discomfort. Anne would try them on when she thought I wasn't looking. That really turned the tables for me. I remember thinking: *Maybe this is exciting. Isn't this what being a woman is all about?*

Anyway, back to the store:

Anne kept on showing me different brassieres. She told me to try a lacy one with ivory rosette inlets on the sides. She insisted I purchase a black satin bra and a sheer, red lacy one! I tried to explain to her that I prefer neutral colors, preferably blush or beige. But she insisted: "If I were you I would buy pink *and* red brassieres!" Mummy was becoming slightly rattled by Anne, but I didn't mind too much. I found her quite amusing! Of course I would like to buy really pretty bras, but I feel that they are meant to be seen, and who sees me in these bras? When I'm a bride I will surely invest in lingerie. But now?

I am not really thinking about boys in that way now anyway…

***

Hitler—why do you hate me so?

The Secondary School is doing a decent job of educating the Jewish boys and girls of Amsterdam. The professors excel in mathematics, literature, and the sciences. But I have a yearning to learn more about my Jewish roots. Since the Nazis have placed such a great deal of emphasis on Jews and Jewishness, I think it is only appropriate for me to learn about Judaism. I know they must hate us all for something— perhaps it is for our religion? I don't see any external differences between myself and other girls my age. We're all struggling with similar issues. Gentile and Jewish girls alike share many of the same concerns. But it doesn't matter. The animosity between Gentile and Jew is growing more and more. What happens in another country no longer remains in another country. I realize that the Dutch are nowhere near as cruel or sadistic as the Nazis, but the Nazis and Hitler's army are the occupiers—so it is their animosity I fear most.

Mazal Alouf-Mizrahi

The Jews have been a hated caste of people since the beginning of recorded history. Ever since they became the "chosen" nation they have inevitably assumed the title the "accursed" nation as well, so much so that Theodore Herzl, the founding father of modern Zionism, thought it best to keep his son's symbol of "Gentile-ness", by denying him the rite of circumcision, the stamp of "Jewish-ness". This stamp on the male body became the burden of proof of his "chosen-ness". (He even went so far as to call him "Hans", a common Gentile name!) But I am not willing to forgo *my* heritage. Father once told me the Franks are a prestigious family, and many of our great-grandparents were quite observant. Perhaps it is the unique messages of our religion that the Nazis find so despicable. I'm rambling…I do that when I have a hard time making sense of things…

I am reading a book now that piqued my curiosity. Sure enough it's a book of questions! Although there are no specific answers to my questions, (which are numerous… can't write them all now…). I found it very interesting. It is titled 'Responsa—Judaism and Jewish Identity in anti-Semitic Europe.' A fellow by the name of Samuel Steiner asks the author, Rabbi Landau, "Do I need to wear a yarmulke at work if I know my co-workers are anti-Semitic?" The Rabbi answered: "Wearing a yarmulke (the dark skull-cap) is only obligatory during prayers, when one pronounces the name of God. If the young man in question feels the yarmulke will in any way threaten his position (as a constant reminder?), then he should refrain from wearing it at all other times, certainly." His answer surprised me. I expected the rabbi to be adamant and insist the man should *not* remove the skull cap. I thought it was intrinsic. Incumbent at all times. I then realized how little I knew of the laws of yarmulkes. Indeed, I didn't know there *were* any! Perhaps I think of the yarmulke like I do my Star of David. One *must* wear it at all times. Jews take grave risks each time they remove it. Judaism, it seems, is not black and white; there are nuances!

I then read another interesting question: "Should one name a child two names, one Gentile and one Jewish to protect the child from anti-Semitism?" Landau answered that it is customary to name a Jewish child in honor of a traditional figure of Jewish lore and the Bible, perhaps a family member (alas my aunt!), perhaps a legendary figure. But in our times it may be positively lifesaving to have a second, non-Jewish name…

The Silent Sister

and although the Israelites in Egypt did not conform to naming their children Egyptian cultural names, one cannot enforce this custom during such dangerous times...

Human life is at stake.

I did not find the answers I was looking for. I wanted to understand the root causes of anti-Semitism.

Without a rabbi to ask, I will have to improvise:

I will now pose my own question, and since I don't have anyone to ask in my room at this very moment (save for the cat, and she doesn't count!), I will try and see if I can answer it on my own. *Why do the Nazis hate us so?* Perhaps the question should really be: *Why do so many Gentiles hate the Jews?*

1. Jews killed Jesus. The Church has, for centuries, blamed the Jews for betraying and murdering their Lord. But many, many individuals (not only Jews) were murdered by the Romans for subversive acts of any kind. The Romans were especially cruel toward those they suspected of political double play or espionage. If that were the case, then the Romans in their own right had an interest in executing Jesus as an organizer. Indeed, Romans executed and crucified (their favorite method most probably) hundreds of unfortunate souls. In any event, I still don't understand why the Nazis hate the Jews. From what I understand, Christ atones for the sins of all Christendom— And he attained this colossal ability due to his death. In that case, all Christians should *love* Jews! (* What a great thought!) Now they can sin *and* they can have eternal forgiveness! The Lord atones for their sins! So the Nazis hate the Jews because (as we stand accused to date) we have slaughtered their Lord, but if their Lord didn't die, they wouldn't have salvation! Perhaps accusing Jews of killing Christ is then simply an excuse to hate Jews and extract revenge? Or perhaps they care not for salvation?

2. The Jews are an inferior race. If we were to go right now to a prison, we would barely find any Jewish prisoners. Jews are rarely imprisoned for rape and murder. Most Jews are family-oriented folk from all walks of life—doctors, lawyers,

merchants. Like any other group of people, Jews are rich and poor, smart and not so smart, pretty and not too pretty, the list goes on. Why are we then deemed inferior? Perhaps because Jews trace their lineage to —? Other Jews! What are the common characteristics of an 'inferior' race? Of course! Thievery, illiteracy, murder, drunkenness? I am not even sure, since I have never considered this before. But I trust the Nazis have painted those pictures of hooked noses for a reason—to debase us all. Only then could they squash us, confiscate our property, and mistreat us. Send us to camps for inferior racial peoples.

3. The Jews are bad luck.
4. Jews smell. (Bad, not good.)
5. The Jews are the cause of world hunger and political instability.
6. Jews don't look like people. They are monkeys. Apes. More akin to vermin than to biped mammals of the human race. I don't know how to respond to this one… all I know is that the last time I saw a picture of Anne and Margot Frank, I must say I saw quite a darling pair of girls!
7. Even God Himself turned his back on the Jews—we might as well emulate Him! The Christians believe the Chosen Nation lost their unique heritage and their birthright; the new nation of Christendom replaced the biblical nation. The very sight of a Jew disproves this theory, and in "righteous indignation" they must demoralize the Jew—in order to regain glory and historical significance.
8. Jews are to be hated. This seems to be the general rule of the day.

***

Jetteke has the flu!

I can't believe someone can be so sick on such a beautiful morning. I went to visit her after Prof. Kahn called her name during attendance, and she did not raise her hand or say her usual 'Thine art here' as if she were speaking in Shakespearean English class (but I believe she confuses the tenses or pronouns). I walked to her house and did not ride my bike because I heard there was more patrol in the main thoroughfare, which is precisely adjacent to her home. (I am a bit fearful of discovery.) Her mother cooked a broth earlier in the day, but she refused to eat. "I'm dying, I'm dying," she croaked. I told her, "You won't die that quickly." She raised an eyebrow and shifted her position on the divan. I offered her soup. At first Jetteke said, "Please! I can't bear the smell of the turnips! I loathe it, but my mother keeps cooking the soup this way!" I decided to feed her whether she enjoyed the turnips or whether she detested them. Thankfully, she did not put up a fight. Jetteke told me I would make a great nurse since I had the patience to hear her complaints without becoming angry or agitated. The truth is that I *do* have a hard time bearing witness to someone else's suffering, and I would *gladly* help someone if he were in need. Jetteke then told me something I did not know—she said I should consider becoming a volunteer at the Medical Center in the center of town—that they were particularly short-staffed. I think I will do just so. If anything, I will volunteer in the maternity ward. There, at least, I will be able to partake in the mothers' elation. And not to mention the newborn babies—who doesn't love a baby? This way I'll vicariously enjoy myself, and I hope to avoid the labor ward as much as possible!

***

Shalom. Ani Yehudiyah. (Hebrew words! "Hello"; "I am a Jew".)

I'm learning Modern Hebrew! I haven't told you enough about my latest interest—the Zionist movement…

I don't recall *how* I became involved in the Zionist movement; I believe I overheard one of the boys mention it in passing at the end of last year. Either way, I've hardly missed a meeting. At first, most of the members would come and go; some would make a ruckus and then leave. Others would find a corner and discuss 'sports.' (Other unmentionables occurred as well. If Father and Mother knew, they would forbid my going. So I shall not report much regarding this.) In short, it was a messy affair. I admit, I barely heard a word at first. The leader, a tall skinny boy with an effeminate voice, would yell, "If you can't keep quiet, leave!" When he was annoyed beyond measure he would bellow, "Shut up!" I observed his behavior (I still cannot remember his name), and I noticed he appeared anxious and insecure. Perhaps for this reason the Zionist Group developed a reputation for noisy interactions at worst and some motivational speeches at best. Part of the problem: no adults. The organization is run by young adults, each eager to make his 'mark' on the world. I believe the oldest member is twenty-five. In any case, Mordechai took over the microphone sometime this past September. He stood out of the crowd for many reasons. Chief among them: his orthodoxy. He is an observant Jew. His yarmulke and his *tzizit*, the stringed four-corned garment, mark his Jewishness, a Jewish star of sorts. His demeanor commands respect: regal, authoritative, and moderately severe; his comportment: serious and intelligent. His dark, short-cropped hair, heavy brows and thick spectacles add to his 'intelligentsia' appearance.

The first words he spoke were not in Dutch, but in Hebrew: "Shalom." He started off his very first speech that first night with a promise: "I promise you all, each and every one of you, that this war will redefine what it means to be a Jew. And by its end, for it *will* eventually come to an end, each Jew will have to determine for his or her own self how he wishes to live his life, fulfill his destiny, as a Jew. I guarantee one thing: we will survive as a people…we will outlive Hitler…and we *will* one day return to Palestine!" Many cheers ensued. Mordechai began his journey into our hearts.

"Our history is a long one…Hitler is not the first to victimize Jews—nor will he be the last. We were blamed for the Bubonic Plague. We were accused of spilling innocent Christian blood for baking matzos. Terrible catastrophes are our fault. The financial depression post the First World War was our fault too. There is no end to nonsensical finger pointing. We are ashamed to speak the Jewish tongue. We are ashamed to call ourselves *Juden*. Let me tell you this today: unless we look into our history, the Bible, for answers we will remain lost … a roaming Jewish star…"

And on and on he spoke.

At times he was poetic and eerily prophetic. (He said it won't take long before Jews retaliate, and news of resistance surfaced soon thereafter.) Many of the younger boys imitate Mordechai, and some, like Peter Schiff (Anne's 'secret' favorite), eventually befriended him. At first I thought Mordechai was thirty; he seemed so knowledgeable and responsible! Baffled, I discovered he is only twenty-two! He is not Dutch-born. Like me, actually, he was born in Frankfurt-am-Main. Mordechai is the youth organizer in the main Jewish Synagogue too. He's invited us all to attend services throughout the year, "not only on the High Holidays," as he cynically remarked. (That's not possible now. The synagogue in the Jewish quarter has been blocked off. He now prays in a building somewhere near Father's office.) He's a fighter. And a philosopher. He loves making fun of our conquerors, "a bunch of criminals in fancy boots and long black coats with guns manufactured by enemies of the Reich!"

Mordechai arches his eyebrows when he speaks of Palestine, and he tends to move his hands quite a bit when he mentions Hitler and the war. I usually sit in the second row to the right during the meetings, the best angle for observation! He fixes his eyes on mine, quite a lot in fact. (I return his gaze.) Jetteke pointed this out. I was too busy returning his gaze to notice that he did not turn his head to the rest of the room as often as a speaker tends to. I can't quite put into words how I feel when I stare at him. His deep-set eyes…. I believe this feeling can best be described as "home-like." I feel I don't need to say much— that he somehow understands me. I fear these 'feelings' are the notions of a "green girl" (an allusion to Shakespeare!). A girl who reads too many books and "reads" too much into her experiences…such an individual needs to be watchful—I hope I heed my own warnings…

I've never seen him relax or eat ice cream at *Oasis*. In fact, he's never lectured seated, even when he injured his ankle. I overheard he enjoys ping-pong though! Supposedly, few have been able to defeat him.

There are MANY rumors about Mordechai. The latest bit of gossip: his family may have been interred in Mauthausen or a different concentration camp in Germany. Supposedly, he was imprisoned in Buchenwald for a few months. I don't know what to make of these morbid tales, and I surely lack the courage to ask him.

It doesn't really matter where he's from. The question is—where is he going?

[Did I mention that many girls think he is handsome?]

***

"Poor Jews!" "What a fate!" "I better stay away from you!" Facial expressions speak wonders.

Lately, I've begun to notice people looking at me with a mixture

Mazal Alouf-Mizrahi

of pity and fear. I believe they pity me because of my classification as 'inferior,' and they fear me because any association with me means they are 'Jew lovers,' a capital offense! I must stop right here and say that many Dutch citizens have placed their very lives at risk trying to help Jews. Unfortunately, the number of people willing to help is dwindling; the Nazi's awful mistreatment (brutal, I've overheard) of 'conspirators' has all but suppressed even the softest hearts and upright souls. Some are sent to Poland and others are executed mercilessly, as sacrificial demonstrations or "examples." Many Gentiles are eager to help, but they are more concerned for their own necks. Many of father's workers are Gentile. I had never thought of them as Gentile per se, but rather as people I happen to know through my father's work. But now I have begun to classify people just as *I* have been classified by the Nazi race mongers.

Before the Nazis arrived people did not even know I was Jewish, but now I blind people with the glare of my emblem and broadcast my race with a very sorry looking Jewish star sewed neatly onto the left lapel of my gray jacket. I wonder why we are meant to participate in a paraded world, where only certain people get to 'dress up' and most people stare them down. Today, I would like to see my neighbors wearing a Jewish star too—for I read that the early Christians were Jews. That means the local bishop should wear a Jewish star in solidarity with Paul (who was Saul), one of the authors of the four gospels. And perhaps the Pope should wear a *streimel* and Hitler should don a pink yarmulke. Now, I know for a *fact* that even Anne would find that hilarious! (She loves a good joke.) I decided he should wear pink because rumor has it his moustache is a mini-wig!

[I even heard rumors that he may be a homosexual. Why would someone who may secretly harbor homosexual leanings discriminate against his own (undeclared) kind?]

Speaking about jokes, I have a good one: what's worse than a Nazi? An Englishman. The Nazis want Europe to be *Judenrein*, and the British won't allow them to escape to Palestine! (And the Americans have placed a quota too.) This is not such a funny joke, but the tragic irony of our situation. Mordechai mentioned this last night (at the meeting of the Jewish Nationalist Group, now known as the Zionist Meeting Group). People chuckled, but there were sad undertones to this 'laughter.' The British released a quota during the worst time in Anti-Semitic history he said. (I didn't know that! I like the British. I hate to think ill of them.) Palestine, he said, is just a new name for the Holy Land, nearly 2,000 years a Jewish homeland. But the Jews were expelled from Judea in 70 AD with the destruction of Herod's temple. I didn't even know the Jews *had* a temple. I was really very dumbstruck and awed at the same time. Father and Mother are not Orthodox Jews, this I know, but I did not realize that there is so much history to our people!

I decided to speak with Mordechai after our session (which lasts past our curfew sometimes). He told me to read *History of the Jews*, by Abraham Abramoff. He actually stopped by today and dropped it off. He stood near the fireplace and placed his arm on the mantle. He overtly admired a couple of photographs of Anne (I believe she's three years of age in those photos). He kept on reiterating that one must "read as much as possible about one's history and legacy." It was as if he was lecturing me, but I wasn't paying too much attention to his sermon. I was too busy staring at his eyes. (Again.) They aren't eyes one sees every day. They seem adrift in an introspective way. To me they state, "I am lonely. I have known too much despair." At the same time, though, I couldn't help but notice a spark of gentle intensity. A paradox of sorts...

He rummaged through his briefcase, which he wears across his body. I noticed a prayer shawl as well as a dictionary.

"Trust me, once you read this book, you'll realize that Jews never belonged anywhere. Not in Germany and not in Spain. Not in Greece or Morocco. Jews are hated everywhere and were even expelled from *England*. Listen to me, read this and tell me if you don't agree that the only homeland for the Jews is *Eretz Israel*!"

Mordechai saluted and left. He smiled warmly before he left for the front door, a hint of his tender heart, I'm sure! He seems very business-like most of the time, though.

Rumors abound, but here are some of my findings regarding the mysterious Mordechai (warning: not as of yet corroborated): he wants to join the secret army of Jewish resistance fighters in Palestine. He also fled Germany after the Nuremberg Laws, but unlike me, he speaks with an accent.

That's about it. As you have noticed, diary, I am not the best detective.

Anyway, he has been organizing these meetings for a while now, but lately he's becoming even more passionate and asking each and every member to organize and recruit new members. I don't know if I will organize myself, but I did inform a few friends from school about our clandestine meetings. Jetteke joined once, but she felt the people there were a little 'unrealistic.' She said the Jews don't have an organized army or even a legal hold to the land. Mordechai maintained that we don't need documents that prove we have a homeland because our history speaks for itself. The Bible is the greatest testimony he said. He then read from the Bible the segment of God's promise to Abraham. The descendants of Isaac, he pointed out, are the inheritors of the Holy Land. Jews have resided and dwelled in Israel since Joshua's conquest; some never left. The vast majority was expelled and wandered the globe. Now is the time to return. He kept on emphasizing this, over and over.

The more I think about what he said, the more I am convinced he is right. What would it be like to dwell in a country where you were the majority and *not* the minority? What would it be like to have a Jewish government? What would it feel like, at the end of a long day, to stroll in the ancient streets, converse in the biblical language with friends, and hear Jewish mothers unafraid to speak Yiddish aloud? I *have* to brush up on my Hebrew! Of course! And I would love to settle in my own country as a citizen, unafraid of dictators like Hitler coming to power and ridiculing us, hating us, wanting us out of their precious Aryan countries. Instead, we'd have our freedom *and* our land. We don't care how big or small it is—if it's ours, we'd gladly live in it!

This all sounds so fantastic, just like a dream! But I recall Mordechai declared, quite fervently, that part of the problem of so many Jews is that they never joined forces and turned this 'dream' into reality. They just sat and bemoaned the loss of the temple, the destruction of Jerusalem, the ruin of a beautiful and sacred city. Eventually, many Jews began to identify themselves with their adopted states until harsh reminders came along: the Crusades, the Inquisition, expulsions, pogroms and now Hitler.

But we don't *have* to feel like victims, he said. Even though we are victimized, we don't need to live out our years as "pathetic landless people praying for an eternal lease on someone else's land." Instead, we should invest in a future where *we can live and die* knowing our children will not have to fear being locked into a ghetto or barred from universities because they had the (unfortunate?) fate of being Jewish.

***

Sunday was *divine*. I played with baby Gaby and roamed by the blustery canals for a good hour. She kept on pointing to the gray geese, squealing, "Birdy! Birdy!" We fed them stale bread, but a patrolman notified me of a "severe fine" if I continued to "disrupt the peace." (Too bad—the geese are hungry, and it's his fault!)

How I love her! The Goslars are our extended 'family,' and baby Gaby is my adopted little sister. How I would have adored a baby in the house! Perhaps my desire for a larger family draws me to Gaby. I don't know.

She sits in the bath and claps her hands each time I play "peek-a-boo." Her chubby fingers remind me of the Sistine Chapel. The cherub's hands... And she giggles. And then I giggle, too! She splashed my hair and hurled her ducky across the bathroom! I thought boys were wild, but I see girls can be spirited too!

On a side point—this past Friday night Hanneli confessed her mother is expecting again! Hanneli hopes her mother has the long-awaited for boy—that would make him the most spoiled boy in all of Amsterdam! I *did* notice she was short of breath lately. Granny mentioned that a pregnant woman breathes shallow breaths to take in more air for her unborn child.

I don't think Mummy will have any more children. I'm not sure if she can.

I don't really think of Mummy in that light, anyway.

Anne thinks Mummy and Daddy don't love one another the same way the Goslars do.

I know Daddy married Mummy when he was in his thirties. Perhaps the romance Anne and I witness in the movies is reserved for young men and women—or perhaps Mummy and Daddy restrain their love before us—Mummy is a modest woman, to say the least. And she is very proper.

I just don't think Daddy and Mummy *have* to love in the same fashion as Hollywood stars to *really* love each other.

Anne disagrees.

Anne is very romantic—she says she will only marry a man who is as unique as Daddy but as handsome as Bogart....

I believe love is an emotion that may begin in a fiery manner, but eventually becomes an eternal ember, more subdued, but more long-lasting as well…

***

The maternity ward and Margot: do they mix?

I took Jetteke's advice seriously and began my first day as a maternity ward volunteer. Sophiia, the head nurse, showed me around the maternity ward. There is a nursery, a labor and delivery department, a surgical room, five linen closets, a reception area, a coffee room, and of course, the postpartum rooms. I believe there are ten maternity rooms in total. Women room together and they remain in the hospital for about two weeks. Men are forbidden to enter the labor department, and children under a certain age must be accompanied by an adult and may visit only at fixed hours.

Dr. Mann, originally from Germany, is an expert gynecologist and obstetrician. The few tufts of hair on his head have all turned gray. He tends to sweat profusely when he is agitated, Sophiia mentioned in passing. He is entirely committed to the new mothers, and he is also an expert neonatologist. The nurses adore him. He hardly returns home.

Most of the nurses work long hours, so volunteers are most welcome. Sophiia insisted, "You don't need to make an appointment." I am simply welcome at any time of the day or night. "The maternity ward is a twenty four hour a day, seven day a week, three hundred and sixty five and a quarter days a year operation. So you are welcome to join the mayhem at any time you so desire." She notified me that the Nazis give a pass to the nurses, so they may leave past curfew. It is not very safe otherwise. She assured me I will receive one if I have to return home past eight o'clock. This seemed very fair. She staggered beside me, dragging her feet, and pointed to the closet with the nurses' uniforms. For some reason the closet is always open. The uniforms are gleaming white and very proper-fitting. She then pinned a note with "maternity volunteer" written neatly in block letters on my right-sided breast pocket. "Do you want one of these?" She held a beaten nurse's 'hat,' yellowed and stained. She read my expression exceedingly well; she immediately returned the item. She pointed to my shoes, "You may want to wear comfortable shoes with rubber soles." I was wearing my fancier pair of heels, to appear office-like. "Not necessary to dress up here…" I made a note of her suggestion. She then held my arm and pointed to postpartum room six— a small room with four beds. "Start your day there. These women gave birth recently. Ask them if they need maternity pads or medication to ease their pain. If so, go to the nurse's station and consult one of the nurses. She will let you know what to do. When you are done, put on gloves and clean the bins. If you have any questions, come see me. I will be assisting Dr. Mann today in the labor department."

I was a bit nervous when I walked into the room, but the ladies quickly put me to work. "Nurse! I need hemorrhoid cream."

"I haven't had my pain medication this morning!" "Please, have someone take my baby to the nursery so I can get some sleep!"

The women looked awful. I felt terrible for them. I ran around the room and back and forth to the station many times that morning. I got a glimpse of a small little one, but I had to run back to clean the bins. I wasn't able to enjoy the baby; more work needed to be done. Some of the mothers asked if I was new. People spot a novice quickly. I was able to speak with one of the mothers, a Mrs. Hershkovits. Most of them were too tired to speak, though. They seemed overwhelmed and somewhat gloomy. I hope the next time I volunteer things will be a bit less hectic!

On my way out, I heard a laboring woman scream in agony. My heart skipped a beat. It was so frightful. It was quiet, and all of a sudden she screeched again. The second time her voice seemed thinner and louder. I heard some more whimpering, and a few moments later yet another shriek. I realized I was exiting the building from the labor department. I quickly made an about face— but not before I heard the ecstatic howl that reverberates in my ear even now as I write this. The nurses were cheering at the same time, and a newborn's hearty cries filled the room, following his first gulp of air as his lungs expanded for the very first time. My heart rate eased after that triumphant sound, and I walked home quickly, ten minutes before curfew, exhausted and inspired.

***

Is an invitation to a festive meal considered an informal 'date'?

Mordechai invited me to an *'Oneg Shabbos,'* a festive meal one Friday evening and Saturday morning. We have eaten by the Goslars *every* Friday night since we arrived in Amsterdam. But I think I will make an exception just this once. Mordechai generally posts flyers by the 'front desk'—a wobbling oak table with three broken drawers—and requests members to sign up for the event. He *particularly* "requested my presence." (Can this be considered a rendezvous?)

Friday nights are usually exciting get-to-gethers. Even though we are not religious we religiously eat by Hanneli's house. On occasion, Mummy and I attend services at our synagogue on Saturday morning; Anne and Daddy prefer to remain at home. This week I will hear Mordechai read from the *Torah*. He wants me to meet him in the makeshift synagogue next-door to the catering hall (by Westermarkt). I heard he is a cantor too. Perhaps he will teach us some Hebrew lyrics and songs; that will be pleasant! Either way, I won't miss this opportunity. I must admit, I am looking forward to it. (Should I borrow a blouse from Mummy?)

I asked Anne if she was interested in coming along, but she is sleeping over at Hanneli Friday night, and she has a previous engagement with a group of girls from school on Saturday. I don't want to spoil her good times. I guess I'll go alone then!

Sometimes I wish Anne were a bit closer in age, perhaps a year or so younger than I. How I would love a companion to confide in! Soon, in a couple of years, Anne will surely mature, but she's mainly a child now. I believe she is going to grow into a sensitive and perceptive young woman. She does point out the foibles of others with such wit! Just the other day I overheard her say that Mummy dislikes her energetic fussiness, but Mummy is no different herself. Anne then pointed out Mummy's tendency to reset the glass armoire every other Sunday morning, just as Anne likes to 'redecorate' her walls every so often with her favorite Hollywood beauties. Just yesterday, in fact, Anne posted a new photo print of Deanna Durbin surrounded by a halo. I noticed that effect, come to think of it, in many American films. Each time the female lead character appears she is suddenly basking in a glorified light, an effect that makes her appear, in my opinion, more like a fantasy of a person than a real woman.

I don't know if young ladies realize that no matter how hard they try, they won't quite achieve this unique effect since it is, after all, an optical illusion of sorts. And they are all so perfectly figured. And some are so thin too! Mummy's friends speak of Loretta Young with such admiration. They confide in one another, "We'll never be beautiful like this Hollywood star or that one…" They seem so apologetic. It is foolish to place too much emphasis on outer perfection, so-to-speak. I think it is for that reason I study so much. I am not ugly, that would be too unpleasant! Youth passes us all by a little too quickly, though. A woman might as well develop her mind, for her body will not last!

Anne thinks I am beautiful, but I don't see a beauty when I look in the mirror. I see a fair girl. With spectacles. Women are beautiful in their youthful years. But their beauty quickly fades. My lot will probably be no different. I was prettier when I was a little girl. The photo in the living room of Anne (probably three years of age or so) and me attests to this. I study that picture quite a bit. Anne seems somewhat lost, and I'm trying to 'protect' her. I admire the depth of her expression. And then I wonder what it would be like to have a daughter all my own. Will she look like me? Will it be difficult to take care of her? Mummy says it was hard for her to take care of such small children— but surely we grew quickly enough! Either way, I'll need a husband first!

Many girls my age have boyfriends. Even Anne has her beaus, but I haven't had the great fortune of 'falling in love.' I don't think it is wise to speak with boys too much, unless they are truly interested in what you have to say, from the standpoint of genuine friendship. Most of the boys (in my class) are terribly obvious in their 'interests.' Of the nineteen, most of them, I'm saddened to report, ogle the girls and enjoy uttering rude remarks. [Mordechai is a bit different, though.] Jetteke has a boyfriend, and so do Henriette and Aleida (obviously). But while I *do* want a man in my life, I want him to see me as a person of depth and not just a female or an object of aesthetics. Sometimes the boys, especially Jacques, say such disturbing things! We girls can't eat icicle pops, chew on pencils, and munch with relish any oblong food article without some boorish comment. I have such a hard time hearing them. Jacques is especially notorious. He degrades the girls daily. Even some of his *pals* think he's too much. I wonder why he behaves this way. Perhaps he doesn't know how to properly deal with his own feelings towards women? Maybe he feels weak—maybe girls make him feel as though they have some type of power over him. Afraid and threatened by their power, he puts us down by reducing us to objects. I can't seem to make sense of his behavior at all! I just hope Anne's 'beaus' are not rude or too forward. They're still young, but that doesn't mean they don't have desires! I have a feeling Anne would reject, at this point, any such impropriety. So, I'm not worried. Father and Mummy don't seem to mind. Mummy trusts us implicitly. I just don't want Anne to get hurt in her relationships.

***

Margot + Maternity ward = ?

Undeterred by the hard work in the maternity ward, I returned to the hospital. Mrs. Strauss had made an impression upon me. I visited her this afternoon. She seems quite lively for a post-partum lady! Her son was born a bit premature, so his head 'slid right through like a fish in jelly.' I was a bit nauseated at first by the imagery, but she laughed it off so heartily I had to join her. Her first-born did not share his brother's small skull, to Mrs. Strauss's great disappointment. Indeed, she labored for twenty-four hours before three doctors were able to dislodge the firstborn's head from the birth canal. Mrs. Strauss related these tales of child bearing with a combination of wit and heartfelt smiles. I imagine this is the way she deals with pain. Either way, she is to remain in the hospital for two more weeks. Her husband came with their firstborn in the evening. Mrs. Strauss adores them both and invited me to visit her at home as soon as she recuperates. 'I think Margot should consider midwifery,' don't you think so, Mr. Strauss?' Mr. Strauss didn't know what to say; he was caught off-guard. 'It is entirely up to the young lady,' he cleverly answered. And I think he is right. I should think it over. I *am* thinking it over, even now, as I write. And it seems lovely to me, but I know there are great difficulties in this field as well. What if the baby's cord is wrapped around his silky neck? The cord is fibrous and quite tough, and such dangers can lead to tragic endings I do not want a part of. What if the fetus turns prior to delivery, and I am unaware of such until an emergency occurs? How will I handle the stress of the moment? Will I be clear-headed, stable, and strong, in control of the situation? Will I become paralyzed by the shrieks of the mother? Will I be able to bear witnessing the mother's pain?

At this point I am not so sure of the answers, but I do know this much: in order to experience the joy of holding the newborn, we must trust a force greater than us all, take the leap into faith and hope for the greatest good. That is the belief I held on to when I heard the mother's shrieks in the labor and delivery room, and that is the belief I hold on to when I visit the nursery and stare at beautiful new babies.

***

Mordechai was right—I enjoyed the *Oneg Shabbos* tremendously. The girls from the Zionist group meetings joined forces and cooked all of Thursday and Friday for our group of thirty-two. (I noticed a couple of girls from Maccabi Hazair attended as well.) They cooked mostly traditional Jewish or "heimish" food. The *kichel* and *cholent* weren't so much to my taste, and the *kugel* and coleslaw were a bit salty. Thank goodness they served *bolas*, my favorite fish dish, Friday night. (Mordechai told me it is a custom to eat fish on *Shabbos*.) Even with the rationing, the girls managed to prepare a banquet.

We met in a dilapidated building near Westermarkt. Before the Nazis sealed off the Dutch Jewish quarter, the new synagogue, the Neie Sjoel, was the synagogue of choice for most Ashkenazi Jews. It was restored in the eighteenth century, so it has an old-fashioned feel. Mordechai directed the youth *minyan* before the occupation of the Neie Sjoel. (But only for a few months.) The building at Westermarkt was vacant, and Mordechai didn't need to pay for its use; it appeared safe, so we met there. Otherwise, I have no idea why Mordechai would choose such a place for a *Shabbos* meal.

The room was very large, but dingy. Cracks on the wall *and* on the floor, peeling paint, a musty odor, and one toilet that didn't flush. The girls tried to dust the room, but no matter what they did it was never clean; it was neglected for too long! The front door did not close properly. The wind from the canals nearby kept forcing the door open. On Saturday, one of the boys found a dead rat. He decided to chase some girls around the room with his treasure. The girls jumped on chairs, shrieked, and one even cried. Mordechai assigned kitchen duties to Rat Boy as a cautionary measure for the rest of the evening.

One of the awkward parts of the evening was the *Kiddush*. I knew when to answer "amen," thanks to my Friday night meals at the Goslars.

But I felt ignorant before all the other girls and boys who understand Hebrew very well. Sytie, one of the Orthodox girls in our group, handed me a prayer book with both a translation and transliteration of the *Kiddush*. Although I heard the *Kiddush* many times before, I never really understood what I was answering "amen" to. Mummy and I attend synagogue on the High Holidays, but we don't celebrate the Sabbath as Orthodox Jews. Father usually reads one of his books… We don't have a "Sabbath meal" during Saturday noon-time. Anne and I play games, go about our regular business…

I never realized there was so much more to Judaism than the High Holidays and the celebration of Chanukah. After we finished our Friday night meal, Mordechai asked us all to sit in a semi-circle. He stood and exclaimed, "The Sabbath is a Queen. And we are her Hosts. The Sabbath has maintained our identity and we identify ourselves as Jews through the Sabbath. Enter Sabbath, Our Queen."

Mordechai explained the meaning of the Sabbath, why Jews observe the day at all. "God created the world in six days, and on the seventh He, so to speak, rested. The Jew is obligated to rest as well in commemoration of the seventh day, in solidarity with the Creator Himself." (This sounds so lofty!) When a Jew rests, explained Mordechai, he indicates to the world that there is, indeed, a Creator. The Jew is forbidden from creating anything new on the Sabbath; codices of Law stipulate that which is allowed or forbidden. (I'm summarizing now.) Mordechai then went on to explain the portion from the *Torah* that he read on Sabbath Day. I love to rest (no problem imitating the Creator in that regard!), but what are these codices of Law? [I'll ask the librarian in school when I get the chance.]

The idea that a Heavenly Being 'rests' is very new to me. What a thought!

Mordechai entertained our group of girls most of the evening. He described Jerusalem. He spoke of the Judean desert and Haifa, one of the port cities in Palestine. "Are there canals in Jerusalem?" Sytie loves the waterways of Amsterdam, but she is eager to move to Palestine. She was only a *bit* disappointed when Mordechai said, "No, but there are plenty of bodies of water in Palestine: the Mediterranean, the Sea of Galilee, the River Jordan, the Dead Sea, and the gulf by the city of Eilat."

"Then there must be coral reefs! I love coral reefs. I read about them in my traveler's manual!" Some girl I did not notice before mentioned this. She was sitting rather closely to Mordechai. I noticed her skirt was a bit short.

"Forget coral reefs. How about trains, electric lines, roads? What's it like there, modern or ancient?

"Palestine is a burgeoning country, and the more European people inhabit the country the more modern it will become."

"So you're saying it is so-so."

"I'm saying it's on the way…"

"What about hospitals—are there doctors in Palestine?"

"I hope you are not a hypochondriac—?"

"No. No. I just wanted to know…"

"Well then, of course!"

And so on.

Mordechai accompanied each member home, to make sure we were all safe.

Before he dropped me off, he asked me if I was hungry.

"Why do you think I am hungry?" I asked.

"Because you didn't eat much."

I felt my cheeks. Yes. They were a bit warm!

"I enjoyed the *bolas*. I enjoyed the desert…"

"It's fine, Margot. I simply enjoy seeing young women eat heartily! There are many hungry children in the world…"

As he said those last lines I detected immense sadness in his eyes—perhaps he knew such children?

"But, it's *Shabbos*. We are forbidden to speak of sad things—so let me say this: I am glad you joined us, Margot. Good night."

We crossed the street, together with Sytie and Bracha, Saul, and Jakob Hirsh. He bowed slightly before I shut the door—very gallant-like…

I thought more about what Mordechai had said on Saturday.

Mordechai approached. He asked, "Are you having a good time?" I said that I was. Surprising me, he said, "Now you see why the Nazis hate us?"

He didn't wait for an answer. "Because we are loyal to God, and we are committed to our customs." (I found that comment interesting and odd at the same time…) "They hate any Jew. If he wears a *streimel*, if he has side locks, if he's modern, if his grandmother was Jewish, his grandfather

Jewish, his great-grandmother Jewish, if he's blind, mute, or dumb—it doesn't matter to them, because at the end of the day, they are not fighting us as individuals, but as representatives of God!"

"If that is the case, then, are you trying to say they hate God?" I asked the question out of sheer curiosity even though the implications are blasphemous.

He smiled this strange smile. "Only the Jewish One."

"Then why do they hate the Polish and the poor Gypsies?"

"Because the Nazis think they are better than them. They want to feel superior, but they are idiots, because they are basically all descendants of the same group of peoples, Indo-Europeans, and later on Celts, Germanic tribes, even Slavs became part of the mixture." Mordechai seemed to have an answer for everything.

"What about the Jews?" I offered.

"They are a group of people no one has much interest in. Hitler needs a great force to unite his people for a common purpose. In order for Germans to overlook the animosity they share for each other, he united his people in their hatred for the Jews. The Jew is Hitler's greatest asset—he will use us all to gain world dominion."

"But I feel almost every group of people found reason to hate Jews. Not only Germans. How do you explain this?"

"Simple. When God singled out the Israelites on Mount Sinai He excluded all other nations. This created the original seeds of anti-Semitism."

I found his answer intriguing. The Nazis hate the Jewish Lord? Perhaps they secretly do. There is no real way to know. How can one find out?

But they most certainly hate the Chosen Nation! Because *they* are not the Chosen Nation. They plan to subjugate us all and turn the tables around, flip the coin: they are the "Aryan Race". They are the Superior ('chosen') Nation. Each time a German woman or man mocks a Jew for his inferiority, they must be feeling their own inferiority keenly. But this knowledge is not something they are aware of, at all! (If Mordechai is right, of course.) And by putting others down, they raise their own sense of superiority. Magically, their esteem is lifted. But must they destroy others in their aim for prominence?

The Silent Sister

Mordechai's words make my head spin round and round. In all my life I never considered these ideas.

I've been hearing a great deal of bitter rhetoric lately. 'We've been chosen to suffer. We're the nation everyone is delighted to NOT have been chosen to be a part of.' 'What good is being a Jew if you'll suffer for it?' I understand these sentiments, but, in all honesty, what do such statements serve? (As I write this, I recall "No one can make you feel inferior without your consent.") It's true. We've been singled out by the leader of another nation and are called vermin and miserable parasites, eager to consume all, but we do not need to add another victory to their battle against the Jews—we should *not* add self-loathing, misery, and self-contempt. It is *they* who should feel contempt at the end of the day! For themselves, for their values and for their leader. I would rather be a despised Jew—a victim—than a victimizer.

Besides, we are not the first to suffer such indignities! Many people have been branded throughout history as the 'OTHER.' This served as an excuse to take advantage of the 'other,' mainly for mercenary purposes. (Do the Germans steal property? I believe they do—how else would they access the resources for their Luftwaffe?) I am sure all of this is too much for my small mind to fully comprehend. But the more I study history, the more I see that tyranny does not endure indefinitely. Surely, Jews are not the first in the line of the oppressed. And I don't believe we will be the last, so long as people have not reformed their hearts.

Either way, Mordechai isn't afraid of mentioning any "radical" notion; he especially enjoys sharing them with me, which I now view as an honor.

"You see that Jewish star he's wearing?" Mordechai pointed at a passerby, an Orthodox man walking with his wife and children by the canal.

"Yes. What about it?"

"That is a symbol of Jewish Pride. One day *Eretz Israel* will carry the same symbol on its flag."

"How do you know this?" I asked, bewildered.

"Very simple. The Jews in Palestine are forging groups of armed resistance, and the Star of David has become the insignia of choice for many in the elite group. It only makes sense that the star is destined to become a national symbol."

The mark of our shame shall become the mark of our glory!

Truly, I gained a new source of strength at that moment. How funny that Mordechai should tell me all of this! How did he know I've been feeling depressed lately? Did he sense my thoughts? Do my eyes reveal my emotions?

In the beginning I was ashamed of my Jewish star. Walking in the street became a humiliating experience. I never felt such indignity. But as I looked around, it seemed half the town was of the Jewish faith. I did not feel alone any longer.

And now, I can add a new inspirational thought: I am *proud* to wear the future insignia of the not-yet but soon-to-be country of Palestine, *Eretz Israel*.

***

How ironic to think that I encountered Mordechai at the hospital! (Was I excited?)

This is how it all happened:

I decided to call Daddy. I wanted to make sure he knew of my whereabouts. I had to walk toward the reception desk, the only station where volunteers may use the telephone. Miep answered and explained that Daddy was at a meeting with Mr. Van Pels. I returned the phone to its receiver and, somewhat disoriented, instead of walking toward the maternity ward—oddly enough—I walked toward the main exit. After a good two minutes I came to my senses. I made an about face. I retraced my steps, and right before me was a man who walked with a strikingly familiar gait. His steps were calculated; he marched with purpose. And then he just stopped. He unfolded a piece of paper and addressed the receptionist:

"I'm looking for a Joseph Hirsh. I could not find him in room 509. Could you be so helpful as to let me know if he was discharged or transferred to another room?"

Mordechai (I recognized his tone of voice immediately) turned, held his face in his large hands and tilted his head in my direction.

He did not recognize me at first. He slightly curled his brow—

"Margot? Margot Frank?" (Of course! My nurse's uniform confused him.)

"Mhmmm." I returned his gaze and smiled.

"Hello, Margot! I had no idea you were a nurse…"

"Excuse me, Sir?" The receptionist seemed annoyed.

"One moment Margot." He held his index finger, just like Professor Kahn, to note that he did not forget me…

"Joseph Hirsh was transferred to room 408."

Mordechai nodded his head. "Thank you Miss."

He turned his full attention to my uniform, and his eyes settled on my upper chest. He read the block letters.

"Oh. So you volunteer."

"Yes. But I am still quite a novice."

"Are you familiar with the hospital, though?"

"Yes. I am." I believe I responded with *over-eager* cheerfulness, quite embarrassing as I think of it.

"Perhaps you can help me find room 408 then?"

I wanted to help him—but my heart skipped a beat, and I really don't know why!

"Certainly."

I can't describe how awkward I felt walking with him without the Zionist crowd. I was incredibly self-conscious. Mordechai couldn't have been more at ease. He seemed very confident and calm.

As we walked past the freight elevators and the nurse's station I began to take note that our conversation seemed a bit strained, which had never happened before. I was focused on my smile—perhaps I had eaten something earlier and bits remained, hiding in the crevices of my teeth! I touched my hair, surely a nervous gesture. Immediately I chastised myself for neglecting my hair this morning—if only I had combed my hair as I usually do and took the time to pin it up! Instead, I ran my fingers through my 'curls' and made good use of Anne's head band. I knew I appeared a bit girlish as I left the house, but I excused my neglectful hair situation on the faulty alarm clock.

And then, the realization that I was wearing my "boy shoes" again (my brown oxfords) caused much unaccustomed consternation. If only I had not listened to Sophiia, who insisted I wear comfortable shoes! And on and on…

"Do you enjoy volunteering?" Mordechai asked. (For a second time.)

Mordechai did not seem to pay too much attention to my shoes. (Thankfully!)

"Yes. I like to take care of the post-partum women. They are remarkable."

"There is a great need for midwives in Palestine. Jewish women, especially amongst the religious sector, are always in need of a good midwife."

I did not respond. I simply listened.

"Did you know that last year alone more than five hundred babies were born in Palestine?"

"No. I never truly thought much about Palestine before our meetings, Mordechai."

We arrived at 408.

"Do you want to meet an extraordinary gentleman?" Mordechai asked.

"Yes, I do."

Mordechai introduced me to Joseph Hirsh. Joseph looks more like an Aryan than a Jew. His eyes are pale blue and his hair the color of dried mangoes. His jawbone is extraordinarily pronounced—you can't help but stare at his mouth. I noticed a dimple on his left cheek as well.

Joseph, it turns out, is a refugee who is now an orphan too. Both his parents were deported to Buchenwald, and Joseph recently learned of their passing. He plans on joining the resistance.

We left the room after fifteen minutes. Mordechai whispered in my ear, "Not a word of what we spoke in that room to anyone. It is for his safety."

Why is he so secretive? Does he have secrets too?

***

"Psst. Jew-Girl. Is yellow your favorite color?"

A child of ten years said that to me today. He is somewhat of an anomaly. Most of the Dutch gentiles feel sorry for us. But I can't help but notice a speck of disgust from some of them as well. I've heard it's worse

34

in Poland. Refugees from Germany, Poland, Belgium, and France are in contact with their relatives back home. Terrible stories surface each day. The Polish resent the Jews and subject them to grave humiliations, especially Hasidim. Poles shave long beards with butcher knives and photograph their debasement of bearded men. Children roam in Warsaw motherless and penniless. Youngsters smuggle goods—they're just so hungry!

I think about the Jews left behind in Germany, the Jews in Poland and in the Ukraine.

What's become of them? I've heard of Jews being burnt alive in synagogues. Can these reports be true?

Why would they burn people in a house of worship? Is sacrilege sanctified by the state? Aren't there laws forbidding such actions?

Mummy and Daddy shield Anne from 'rumors' (as Mummy prefers to refer to them) to spare her dreadful nightmares. I think Anne ought to know, at least a little bit, about the woes afflicting our people. Not because I want to worry her, but because I feel it is important that she is not shocked if she were to hear terrible reports (perhaps exaggerated) from outside sources. It is all too much for anyone to bear, let alone a gentle soul like Anne, but we cannot afford to live in naiveté. Not today.

***

Will you lend me your spectacles, Mordechai?

I feel this yearning inside me to breathe the air of Haifa, a city Mordechai swears is surrounded by the most beautiful mountains and captivating Mediterranean beaches. He showed us photographs of Tel Aviv. He promised us it would one day look like New York City! I can't believe that! But he says he has the vision, so if we don't, just trust him. 'I'll gladly lend my spectacles to anyone brave enough to borrow them!' He is not afraid of speaking his mind.

He showed us some of the streets of Jerusalem before European Jews arrived (sometime in the early 1880's) and the way it looks today. I must admit, it seemed quite romantic. Little alcoves, cobble-stoned pavements, olive trees sprouting in the middle of a dirt road. And of course, the Western Wall. He says Jews cannot pray there since the territory is surrounded by hostile Muslims, but he pledged that one day Jews will offer supplication *without* fear for their lives. I asked him why the Wailing Wall was considered 'holy.' He then told me the most fascinating thing: it is the actual wall that surrounded the Temple in the time of Herod, and it still exists *today*! The surviving wall. Stones as old as Solomon perhaps, if one were to dig deep enough. Slabs as thick as years and years of executions and expulsions, inquisitions and crusades. The doves come and perch atop stones of ancient times, the same stones that witnessed the slaughter of the priests during the final battles for Jerusalem. These stones are testament, surely, of the Jews' right to settle the land. The Wailing Wall.

Each Jew is a wailing wall, is he not? We will survive this terrible time! A wall that bears witness to the millennia of intolerance and cruelty to our people bears witness today that the Jew is in grave danger.

"The wandering Jew doesn't need to wander anymore," Mordechai loves to say. And he's right. We don't need to rely on people who hate us to be kind to us. Even if only a few hate us, as long as they are the ones who control us, then our lives will be threatened. Our future's at risk. I firmly believe that after this terrible war is over I will immigrate to Palestine. Maybe in 'Eretz Israel,' as Mordechai likes to say, I will be able to raise my children in safety and with peace of mind. Maybe in *Eretz Israel* I will feel fulfilled as a woman and as a Jew. Maybe in *Eretz Israel* my sister and I will find that wearing a Jewish star is not a symbol of shame but of national pride. Just maybe, in *Eretz Israel*, people can plant a tree knowing their grandchildren will eat its fruit.

***

Today, Germany and Europe are overrun by puppets blindly mimicking the movements of the puppet maker. Rifle up. Down. March. Forward. Stop. Arm. Rearm. Battle. Fire!!

Beat. Humiliate. Shout!

Daddy says *Mein Kampf* is nothing but the ramblings of a madman. That matters little. Publishers have printed the book for all the eager readers of Germany and European countries sympathetic to Hitler's cause. In some circles it has replaced the Bible. Hitler has replaced Jesus, and Berlin is the New Jerusalem. Nazism has metastasized across Germany and into Austria. We thought we'd escaped the Nuremberg Laws for good when we left Germany—but here they are, taunting us in Amsterdam, once a city of religious tolerance. Father says we are to go into hiding. He is slowly taking care of the arrangements. (He planned this from nearly a year ago, I believe.) He thinks we have a greater chance waiting out the war. It can't last that much longer. So he says. I don't know. Father is wise. He is optimistic.

Pim is usually optimistic, unlike Mr. Goslar who hates the Germans and expects the worst. "You shouldn't put any trust in the Germans, Otto." I've overheard their conversations on numerous occasions; (Daddy's point of view is far more pleasant than Mr. Goslar's.)

Father has not told Anne just yet. Mummy informed me earlier today. It hasn't sunk in yet. Life is somewhat normal. Anne and I occasionally meet friends after school in *Oasis*...

Mummy and Father stroll in the park on Saturdays. Anne plays backgammon with Hanneli, and she sails the ferry with her friends. For life to stop so suddenly and for an indefinite amount of time seems hard to swallow. Perhaps even impossible! We won't be able to walk outdoors! I can only imagine the circumstances of such living conditions. Mummy says 'her Otto' has always been resourceful, and she knows he will take care of all the details. Mummy seems a bit dazed when she looks around the house, I have come to notice.

Anne's confused. She doesn't understand why Mummy rummages through closets and armoires daily. Father specifically exhorted me *not* to break the news to her just yet, to give her as much carefree time as possible. "Because soon enough she'll have to grow up." Goodness! Anne will find living in closed quarters akin to drowning! Such a suffocating experience; she breathes the outdoors more than *anyone* else I know. Even in winter she plays, sometimes for hours, in the snow, carousing with her friends. Wool mittens, a warm scarf around her nose, a fuzzy hat, warm boots, and she's set. She is never indoors during the long, sultry days of summer! What will she do? From what I understood we may not be alone. Father says the plans are as of now "slightly premature." So be it!

***

What excitement! I played ping-pong with Mordechai. What an exhilarating match!

I have been in the habit of playing ping-pong as a way of diffusing the anxiety that inevitably accumulates. I probably began playing in earnest about a year ago. (I previously loved tennis, but I now prefer ping-pong.)

Jetteke usually meets me and plays a set or two. Sometimes I play with Hanneli. We enjoy strolling with Baby Gaby. If she is sleeping in the stroller, we simply take her along to the courts and have a grand time.

But today was different. Jetteke wasn't feeling well again, and Hanneli had to take the baby to the physician. (She is coughing too much lately!)

I thought to myself, "Just go and play. There is always someone searching for a partner."

Sure enough the court was busy. As fate would have it, of all the boys in Amsterdam—

Jacques!

Jacques was playing a round with a boy I did not recognize.

Each time our eyes met I couldn't help but feel uneasy. I imagined he was piercing through my blouse and past my brassiere. I folded my arms and stood by the corner gate.

"Ah. Margot! Are you interested in playing the next round? This dunce is sure to lose, just wait and see!"

Jacques is a competitive player, but his habit of staring at a woman's chest is his tragic flaw. He lost the game! I suppressed a giggle when he banged his racquet on the table demanding a replay.

"Would you like to take his place?" The unidentified boy turned to me and spoke rather lazily.

I agreed. "Sure."

He introduced himself.

"Abraham Klein."

"Margot Frank."

And we began. Abraham is an amateur player, I quickly took note. He utilized the same form, and he did not like to move around too much. He had good focus, though.

I did well for the most part until I saw Mordechai with some of the Zionist boys and girls. The group walked toward the table and surrounded the court. Mordechai inched toward the ping-pong table and stood behind me.

"Swerve to the left, and he will be caught completely off guard, Margot."

I listened to Mordechai and went on to win a clear victory!

Abraham seemed quite impressed. We shook hands.

"Nice game. Hopefully I'll see you here again next week?"

"Perhaps."

"Nice to meet you."

"Likewise," I said.

Mordechai gently removed the racquet from Abraham's hands and said in a booming voice,

"Well, then, Margot. You know what this means?"

I turned to glance at him. His sleeves were rolled up. He placed his *yarmulke* in his pocket. He tightened the laces of his shoes.

"Are you ready?"

Of course! Mordechai was keen for a match!

I can't begin to describe how weak I felt—and it was all so sudden! A spasm of vertigo gripped me for a few seconds; I wiped my hands on my kerchief at least five times. I was out of breath, and we didn't even begin!

He positioned himself where Abraham had stood five minutes earlier. He stood with his legs akimbo and lowered his mid-section by a couple of centimeters. He was poised. Ready for the first "attack."

"Winners serve."

I swerved the ball toward the right of the table, but the ball hit the net.

"Don't worry. I don't believe in beginner's luck!" He chuckled.

Again, I tried to serve. My eyes were fixed on the position of his thighs. They seemed as though they were almost parallel with the ground.

(I noticed a butterfly and focused on its wings. They were bright yellow. Butterflies never live too long. I had that thought—very strange, no?)

I served well. He returned with a strong thrust of his wrist. The ball went over the net and –bam! I managed to hit the ball with precision. He failed to anticipate my return…the ball disappeared off the table! And on and on we played.

Hit; miss. Win one, lose another. I lost track of the score after a while. I began to understand the concept of "It's how you play the game." I learned how to serve with even force, to match Mordechai's aggressive returns.

I listened and closely watched for any sleight of hand—if he wanted me to "think" that he was going to hit the ball to the right and truly intend for the left...

How strange: we did not speak throughout the entire event.

I wanted him to notice that I was unafraid to lose; that I valued the sport; that I was a cheerful competitor who knows how to handle a tough situation well.

After a good fifteen minutes, the crowd cheered. Mordechai had clearly won. I can't recall the score. I was too focused on Mordechai's techniques.

Mordechai is a superior player. Secretly, I'm proud of him. Even if it means I'm the "loser."

"Wonderful match, Margot!" Mordechai was almost panting, and when he stood to congratulate me on my performance I felt his hot breath on my face.

"Would you like a glass of water, Margot? Perhaps the vendors sell a refreshing drink?"

He was genuinely concerned.

"Why do you think I need one?" I asked.

"Because you are quite flushed, Margot."

At this point I felt quite drenched. And my throat—parched.

"Margot, sit down over there. (He led me to a bench.) I'll fetch a drink. One moment."

He ran to the nearest vendor. I felt overwhelmingly alive. My hands were shaking a bit. My blood was boiling through the most intimate crevices of my body. I sat there contemplating the promise of a cool drink... and maybe even more!

I was immensely attracted to the warmth of Mordechai's hot breath. I began to feel sensations throughout my entire body, feelings I had never sensed before.

I knew Mordechai fueled my raging thoughts, and I tried as hard as I could to suppress them.

I rested my head in my hands, cupped my temples with tender care and silently fought to regain my composure.

I concentrated on the promise of a soothing cup of water.

I felt my temples beat, loudly, just as I sensed the most intimate parts of my body beat with an incredibly raw and new rhythm.

I silenced my heart and cooled the throbs of such bittersweet, new-found wonder.

I closed my eyes and commanded my blood to boil with less urgency to cool the heat of the mysterious source that held me in its thrall.

I stood as Mordechai approached. I neatly reconfigured the pin-tucked folds of my skirt.

I drank the cool beverage—with my eyes staring intently into Mordechai's. I barely whispered a "thank you" before I returned home with a longing to confide in writing what I feared to admit to myself only moments ago…

***

Lately, I have a hard time living at ease knowing that the routine of our lives will dramatically change. Anne is as carefree as ever. She is already speaking of her birthday, which is not for another month. At least I can be glad for her. One or two of her friends (she has many, I have a hard time keeping track of them all) left Amsterdam for Switzerland. Many Jews are arranging some sort of escape plan. Some are relying on Dutch Gentiles for help. Others are heading to England (if they are lucky enough to obtain a visa). Most Jews plan to remain on the outskirts of Amsterdam or in the vicinity of the city. They hope to evade the Gestapo. Jetteke confided that she plans to hide; she swore me to secrecy. Even though her parents are sickly, they want her to keep as far away as possible from her home. Jetteke is torn: she feels she is duty-bound to care for them, but she must obey their wishes as well. She all but cried when she revealed her misgivings. "I think you should listen to your parents. They will take care of each other." She nodded her head, and a tear slipped down her cheek.

***

Bad news: Father says I must adhere to the curfew!

A couple of young men were imprisoned for remaining outdoors past the curfew. Up until now Anne and I have not been so meticulous with keeping to curfew. I volunteered until 10pm only this past Monday night. (I had the nurse's pass, but Father doesn't want me to take any chances.) Mummy is worried stiff. I caught her biting her lovely nails the other day. Rumors of brutal treatment and imprisonment reached Mummy's ears yet again. Father is more optimistic and in control of his emotions. Mummy is anxious. She keeps reorganizing the front closets. It is as if her life depends on a neat home. She frets over Anne's 'clutter' and admonishes her, sometimes needlessly. I'm distraught too, but I'm in school most of the day so I am still sheltered. I hear Mummy rummaging through the cupboard in the middle of the night. She's been drinking a great deal of coffee lately. Father repeatedly exhorts Mummy: "Don't speak too much to your friends!" They worry her with horror stories. I overheard Father say a bit harshly: "Refrain from mentioning anything before Anne." He was adamant; Mummy promised to keep quiet.

Mordechai has the *opposite* attitude! He speaks freely of the ghettos and horrors in Warsaw and other cities throughout Europe. "The Jews are a problem, a menace. The Nazis want to revert to the Middle Ages and ghettoize the Jews. Hitler's greatest enemy is not Communism but the feeble Jew! Our lease on this land is over, my friends. It's time to return to *our* Fatherland!" Many of his friends clap their hands. A few begin to sing the 'Hatikvah.' I feel overwhelmed when I hear his words. I am beginning to feel that Amsterdam is less of a home. Although Amsterdam is so very beautiful and the city has been hospitable for many generations, the Nazis have left a bitter taste in our mouths. I fear the worst even as I pray for the best.

The Nazis have destroyed too many people's lives. And it is just too bad! My life here could have been just as pleasant as any other person's—were it not for these wretched Nazi megalomaniacs! Europe is becoming, slowly but surely, an extension of Nazi Germany proper. At night the city appears more like a town of invisible inhabitants than the vibrant and lively place I love. Papa says evil cannot endure. He doesn't speak much of the war, but he plans to escape very soon. I overheard him speaking to Miep, "We must be extremely wary with whom we share this information…in the warehouse…for the remainder of the war…it won't last…" We will have to enlist the help of Gentile friends, no doubt, for the success of his plans.

I believe Papa has made a sound decision. Perhaps Switzerland will be conquered and we are delaying the inevitable. Here we have acquaintances… we have provisions… we have a warehouse…

I don't know what else to think.

Papa knows best.

***

I confided in Mordechai today that I want to live in Palestine after the war. He is the only one who knows. I didn't even tell Mummy or Jetteke.

I am usually so reticent; I have no idea why I did so. He was supportive, to say the least! "Palestine is your homeland. But you must also be *prepared* to live there." He then asked me, "What are you going to do there?" Of course! What a practical question. I didn't answer him, but I must say such practicalities completely eluded me. What will I do there? Well, what would I have liked to accomplish in Amsterdam were there no such thing as this wretched war?

I considered becoming a doctor, but I don't know if I want to dedicate myself to such rigors, which may take me away from caring for my own children and husband. I love children! I want to have as many as I can take care of. But I also love physiology and anatomy. I study these subjects when I have had enough of mathematics and physics. I am especially intrigued by pregnancy. There is a photograph of a fetus in the womb (the woman was dead, unfortunately) inside one of the tomes I borrow from the library. Many people would be disgusted or perhaps even frightened by the very sight of the thing, but I was completely in awe. I now look at every pregnant woman with much admiration. So many walking miracles, yet we fail to acknowledge them every day! I love to see the expression of the newborns in the hospital: they look like old people! But they are so tiny and pure.

The mothers are exhausted, so the newborns spend much time in the nursery. I volunteered there a couple of times, and I can't believe how much fun I had taking care of the little ones! The mothers' ashen skin is marked with popped veins and some have dark rings beneath their eyes. Many complain of hemorrhoids. When I dispense the maternity pads and hemorrhoid cream, they respond with gratitude—*this* is what makes them happy! Sometimes they will moan and say the reverse contractions are worse than the labor itself. I then dispense, together with a nurse by my side, strong drugs to ease their pain.

Some women become a bit saddened after the delivery of their baby. Even though the baby is healthy, the mother is not always very happy! This seems very odd to me, but I believe it is a result of the difficult time they went through the entire pregnancy and now the pain of the labor— for many, the pain overwhelms their sense of appreciation and joy. Perhaps there is a way to better ease their pain, and not only with medication? If midwives were more like mothers and sisters throughout the pregnancy and after the delivery, perhaps if women didn't feel isolated in their misery, perhaps *then* we would see fewer cases of such unhappiness? I really don't know, but I believe some changes need to be made. I also don't understand why these women are in a hospital. It seems such a cold place to give birth to such darling little ones. Perhaps some music and greenery would benefit the postpartum women. Overall, volunteering in the hospital has opened my eyes to the difficulties every woman faces: we want children, but the process is so very painful!

I overheard Henriette tell Aleida that the first time is almost as terrible as childbirth. The hymen is a very tough, fibrous tissue and in a very sensitive area, so I deduced this must be true. Yet this doesn't stop women from making love…and the pain of childbirth doesn't deter them from bearing children. Today women use different forms of birth control, I know that. I saw a condom in a pharmacy once, behind the counter, in a clear container. (It didn't look particularly aesthetic; it seems very functional.) I was a bit embarrassed because I particularly recalled a woman in the hospital swearing that she'd make her husband wear two the next time he wanted to share her bed! That woman looked very frail to me, but she has four children, from what I understand. It all seems so strange to me. What powers does a man possess that enables a woman to ignore the possibility of incredible woe and pain? I cannot fathom the pleasures, but they must be enormous.

It seems my heart is with the expectant mothers. My heart fills with enthusiasm each time I visit the maternity ward and each time I hold a newborn's tiny hand in mine. I wish to surround myself with such sources of life—*my* entire life!

So I think I know what I will do in Eretz Israel.

(How I long for that moment when I will become a "we" in the deepest sense, but hush!)

***

The Germans are advancing into neighboring countries with frightening celerity. "You need not fear the maelstrom of Germany, my loyal citizens. The Allies will, with God's help, advance into Holland very soon. The tide may turn just yet. Have faith." The Queen's words offer a spark of hope. The truth is harder to tolerate. Day by day more and more conquered territories carry Nazi flag posts. Jews are the first targets of assault. They are rounded up at every opportunity. Little mercy and much brutality is the natural order. Ghastly tales are surfacing, and we don't know what to make of them. People, especially the Dutch, don't believe "crazy" stories of starvation, disease, ghettoizing or routine "roundups" to undisclosed locations.

The labor camps are no secret. We've all heard of Amersfoort, but we don't know what really happens there. (Mordechai speaks little of Buchenwald, so I am beginning to doubt the veracity of the rumors.) People constantly try to boost their morale, "Oh! The Germans are the most sophisticated of all Europeans. They are making good use of their labor force. Rumors cannot be sustained." On the Ferry I heard a new remark this morning, "Hitler may despise the Jew, and he may aspire to world domination, but he has Churchill to reckon with." Mummy tends to say, "We're in the twentieth century. Why would the Nazis turn back the clock? We're no longer in the seventeenth century! Jews don't live in ghettos anymore." Prof. Kahn says, "It is illogical to eradicate a social force of good. Jews have, for most of this century, contributed to all the sciences, mathematics, and medicine. Simply think of Einstein, Freud, Otto Loewi. All this racial finger pointing will eventually prove fruitless. People will regain their senses." Prof. Steiner: "Jews have been the target of odium for as long as anyone can remember. This too shall pass and perhaps haunt us again. We must weather the storm today and strengthen our children for tomorrow."

I don't know what to believe. I fear the worst. I have this awful feeling we are blinded by our desire to hold on to our lives, our routines, our comforts. Besides, who can make sense of our enemy? Perhaps our ignorance is our greatest enemy.

And perhaps our belief in the goodness of man may prove our undoing as well.

There is no way to know—and that's worse than knowing.

✲✲✲

"We are likened to the dust—and to the stars." Mordechai began his speech this evening on a melancholy note. He seemed resolute as his voice drifted. The meetings are packed with boys and girls as of late. Many sit on the floor and even more stand behind the last row of chairs. (Even Maccabi Hazair didn't boast of such numbers!) This evening most members left with tears in their eyes and, oddly enough, hopeful smiles on their faces. I have never felt such awesome inspiration before.

The room was stifling. Mordechai had difficulty gaining control of the podium. He repeated himself several times, "We are likened to the dust and to the stars." After a few minutes, he was able to continue.

I summarize: "We can be trampled upon. If we forsake our identity, if we allow the Bible to become just another book collecting dust on the shelf, then we are likened to the dust. We can become in the eyes of the world insignificant like the dust of this earth. If we forsake our identity. If we refuse to live out our destiny. If we allow the Bible to become an ancient scroll with little connection to our daily lives, then we will be stomped upon. Like the dust of the Earth." (Many found this segment slightly offensive. Some boys began to boo, but Mordechai continued despite the noisy interference.)

He raised his voice:

"For it is the Bible that tells the story of our Exodus from Pharaoh's enslavement. For it is the Bible that describes our ascent from a lowly group of people into a scholarly and princely nation. We cannot afford to forsake our legacy as Jews. We must heed God's words and pay careful attention to His counsel. Do not be ashamed of your roots. A Jew may be lowly today, but he is destined to rise again tomorrow." (Mordechai regained footing at this point.) "If we stand proud and proclaim our enduring promise to the Lord of The Jews, to be a guiding Torch in an everlasting fog, then we will become the Nation of the Star.

Our Enemies have already proclaimed their defeat. Look at your dress! You don the Star of David; you proclaim your kingship and your royal ancestry! They do not *know* what they ask of us when they command us to wear the Jewish Star. The enemies of God, of the Jews, and of all Humanity, have succumbed to us! They are, in the least, demonstrating to us, the Jews, how to win this battle against God and the People of the Jewish Lord: retain your dignity as a Jew and your embers will never cease to illuminate the universe!"

Many were stunned into silence. We have felt shame and disgrace, as a people with a mark, a stain, on our clothes. The Star of David was neither a prize nor the proud insignia of 'chosenness'. Tonight, our perception changed. We felt elevated. Resurrected. We regained our sense of purpose.

Mordechai sensed the air of defiance and pride in the air. He continued.

"We all fear the worst. The enemies of our God, the One God of Abraham, Isaac, and Jacob, the God who slew the Egyptians in the Reed Sea, the God of Moses, and the God who hears the cries of widows and orphans, trample upon our brothers and sisters. They yearn to turn us all into dust! But even as they desperately try to nullify the great significance of the Jew, the greater they try to eradicate us all, the more our dust will turn into sparks of light, our embers into flames, our tears into wellsprings of joy. Individual sparks will congregate and illumine the darkness of this continent, a light with such intensity, no man's eye will tolerate."

"The Jew is Eternal. So long as the Lord of Israel is One, His people shall roam this Earth. Hitler cannot outwit God; Hitler will not outwit the Jews. No matter how demonic his plans for us all, God has greater plans. God stood alone before creation and after creation. He will remain One after the chaos of this war is over. Have faith in the Lord of Israel in the face of faithless brutality!"

Many began clapping hands at this point. Mordechai held up his hand. He had more to say.

"The World will learn, yet again from the Jews, that a world without God in our midst, is a world bereft of all humanity. Have mercy prevail. Show compassion when cruelty is palpable as the roof of your mouth; demonstrate kindness, when viciousness threatens to eradicate all hopes of a better future.

And even in the face of great peril, do not fear that you have lived in vain— for we are the Generation of the Star— our Light will illuminate the cosmos for all Time to Come. Amen."

Some girls cried and even hugged Mordechai. He was stunned at the outpouring of emotion. He then began to sing, "Israel is yet alive. Israel is yet alive. David, King of Israel, alive, alive and alive!" He sang in Hebrew and in Dutch. The religious boys joined. Some girls danced the hora.

A young man began to fiddle. I cleared the chairs. The girls danced in a circle. Someone brought a prayer book and held it high, as boys clapped their hands. "Israel is yet alive!" We repeated this refrain hundreds of times. Sytie grabbed my hand and helped me join the girls' dance. I followed their motions. I became dizzy from the circling motion. "Come! The boys are raising Mordechai on a chair!" Sytie grabbed me again, and we stood watching the boys raise Mordechai up and down up and down. "Alive, alive, and alive!" With each word, they raised him AAAAAAALLLLL (up) IIIIVEEEEE (down.) He beamed and clapped his hands the entire time. I stood on a chair at one point for a better view. Then, from the left side of the room, five boys linked shoulder to shoulder danced toward Mordechai just as five boys to the right did the same. In and out, up and down. It was fun to watch! Mordechai's eyes caught mine, and I felt the noise pause and the silence break. 'Thank you.' I tried to tell him, but I don't know if he read my expression, since I had not uttered a word the entire evening.

I am overwhelmed by it all. The Generation of the Star? The Jew is eternal? I had never given my identity such *deep* thought. I have much to think about tonight before I fall asleep.

***

A Nazi guard spit in my eye today.

I can't seem to get over the degradation. I have done nothing to this man. I was standing by the corner of the bank…He saw my star…he had such hatred in his eyes! I quickly crossed the street and thanked God I wear spectacles—for I surely would have more to rinse out! I showered quickly, and I am now wearing my pajamas. I feel completely robbed of my dignity. I kept on looking at my face in the shower, in the reflection of the glass doors, to try and understand what was so terribly hateful about me. I know I have not harmed anyone nor have I caused pain intentionally to any person I know. Perhaps being Jewish is the ultimate offense. My face is so Jewish, even if he did not see my star he would have spit with spite. So many people on this small planet hate Jews, so many hate me. Yet I do not hate them! What is it about me that they hate so much? One man cannot inspire hatred in so many men and women if the hatred was not there to begin with. For generations Gentiles have conspired against Jews, and today one man showed his malice and disgust for a 'Jewess.' Yet I believe I am dignified, and I am proud of being a Jew. I am proud of my ancestry and of my values. I know it is the Jew who taught the world 'Love thy neighbor…' Do not upon others…' I know it is the Jew who taught the world the very concept of ethics and moral culpability. The early Christians learned basic civility from Jewish texts. It is the Jew who taught the world 'Do not covet' and 'Do not commit Adultery.' Perhaps this hatred is not really intended toward me personally but toward what I represent? This hatred seems to be geared at what *my people represent* rather than who I am as a person. (I just cannot make sense of all of this any other way—for I don't know this man and he doesn't know me…)

Perhaps this Nazi guard would like to live a life without conscience, without morals, and I am a reminder that he cannot live a life free from moral culpability? The sense of what is right and what is wrong weighs heavily on the shoulders of many. Why not eradicate this heaviness?

The very presence of the Jew, especially the Hasidic Jew holding unto his Torah scroll, inflames the Nazi masses. In Europe there is a new crusade in the name of Hitler. It is called Nazism but perhaps it should be called Anti-Godism. For I know that Hitler probably doesn't hate the Jew so much as an individual but rather as the symbol of a force that burdens him with a conscience. And who chose the Jew to represent the burden of good and of God's ways? God Himself! The 'infidels' are waging war on the people of the book, on the chosen nation, on the representatives of the Lord. Yet nowhere has there been mention of religion; but what is this war against the Jews if not a religiously inspired war? Hitler needs the masses of Germans to aid him in his conquest for world dominion. (Mordechai says this all the time, and I am beginning to believe him wholeheartedly.) Which force binds people? What force can compel a people of various backgrounds to gather and expel another group? The age-old force of religion. But it is veiled in a new cloth and a new name (Nazism). Why not inspire them all with an age-old hatred towards Jews and the Bible they stand for? Aren't we the ones who killed their Lord? For so long they have seen us all as an impediment. For so long they have put up with the Jewish thorn. Now is the time to weed out this thorn! So this guard will spit at me, and he will teach his son to spit in my face too, but what these people don't realize is that this hatred will inevitably cause them even greater shame than the shamelessness of their hatred.

***

Amsterdam meets Warsaw.

Mordechai asked me to sit near him tonight. At first I was a bit hesitant, but I did so out of respect. (I think.) I admire his passionate energy, his resolve. His smooth forehead. His eloquence.

But I don't want rumors to circulate about the two of us…I don't want to give the wrong impression… perhaps that was the cause of my hesitation.

But, by and by, I brought my chair closer to his. No one seemed to take much notice.

He asked me what I thought of his speech. I didn't want to show *too* much admiration. So I told him, "I believe you spoke well." I have a hard time conversing with people freely, especially if they are not friends or family. But I believe he was pleased enough. And by now Mordechai is a friend. (*Why do I need to dissect such matters?)

There was a ruckus tonight. Mordechai had a hard time quieting the group, more so than usual. A man who escaped from the Warsaw ghetto joined our group and he was causing much upset. He spoke in a combined German-Dutch-Yiddish-Polish. I believe this is what he said: "The Germans are ruthless. There are rumors of mass shootings in Belarus…the conditions are deplorable…people are dying by the hour…"

"Who are you?" One boy asked.

Peter Schiff pulled me aside and asked me if I knew the man. One girl was crying hysterically in the corner, rocking back and forth. I later learned she has relatives in Poland. Most of us listened in shocked disbelief.

"Why would the Nazis shoot innocent people? What would they gain from this? Don't they need people for their factories?" Peter asked the man.

The man, who wore such tattered clothes I was tempted to run back home and give him Daddy's cast-offs, looked beaten. "I don't know why. Does it matter? This is the situation!"

"You're lying!" "I don't believe you!"

Back and forth, the poor man tried to convince a group of adolescents that their conquerors had more of an interest in seeing them dead in some ditch than alive, going about their business. Mordechai led him by the shoulders to the adjacent room. He prepared him a cup of coffee and spoke to him in Yiddish. I don't know what he told him, but the man quietly left. I later asked Mordechai what occurred between the two of them. "I simply told him that frightening them with stories will not lead to any good. People cannot grasp what a Nazi is capable of. Instead, I provided food, clothes, and some money and urged him to speak with the Jewish council. I told him that I would speak to the group about escaping or hiding from the Nazis without mentioning you or what you have said."

Truth be told, Mordechai spoke urgently tonight. He implored us to "try and avoid deportation to Poland or Germany. Urge your families to seek visas to Brazil or Australia. Do not allow the Nazis to frighten you into submission!" Two sisters sat in the back of the room holding hands with a fierce grip. They were from a poor family, and their father passed on two years earlier. They do not have the means to escape, from what I understand. They left the meeting trying to console one another. I don't know if they succeeded.

The Warsaw refugee sneaked into the backroom at the end of the evening, when most of the members left. I had my nurse's pass, so I remained to clear up a bit. I phoned Father to let him know I would be twenty minutes late. I assured him I had the pass, just in case a guard would detain me. The refugee approached me; he spoke in broken Dutch, which sounded more like German. "Do you have relatives in Poland?" Before I got the chance to speak to him, Mordechai ushered him into his 'office.' The poor man probably needed lodging. Mordechai saw to it all, I'm sure. He has many connections in town. To my surprise, Mordechai insisted on walking me home. We locked the doors to the "Town Meeting Hall" (aka Zionist Meeting Group!), looked both ways furtively, and began pacing towards our street.

"I had the pleasure of meeting your sister Anne, Margot," he said.

"Oh. How so?"

"I met her at a friend's house. She's a cheerful young lady. She looks a lot like you too."

"We have the 'Frank' stamp. When we were little we were known as the 'Frank sisters.' But now we are in different forms in school, so we have different teachers and acquaintances."

"Are you close?"

"Not really. She's three years younger, so we share different interests. But we love each other…"

"You should stay as close as possible. This war has torn many families apart."

"What about you? Do you have family in Amsterdam?" My curiosity was palpable.

"I know there are rumors about my family. I have two sisters. My father died in Germany when I was young. My mother is with my sisters. They are, as of now, detained in Westerbork."

"The transit camp?" I asked.

"Yes. My family is considered German refugees."

Silence. My family could have been in the same situation had we not left Germany before the war.

"I was born in Frankfurt-am-Main." I volunteered.

"Anne informed me. So you are not Dutch-born; but I barely detect an accent!"

"My friend Jetteke says the same. We moved when I was still a young girl, so I learned the language quickly. How about you?"

"I am a quick study when it comes to languages too. I studied Dutch in Westerbork for a couple of years. I managed to leave the camp with an ID card from a guard. I "bought" the card with twenty cigarettes. Do you want to see it?"

The identity card was not stamped with a J. No wonder he did not fear the police and no wonder he walked around without the Jewish Star. This now occurred to me as I noticed he was not wearing one. The card read 'Herman Groesbeck.' Mordechai's picture was perfectly marked, molded into the card. On the side of the card "Dutch Labor Force" was fixed with cursive pink ink.

"So, you are Herman when you leave the group and Mordechai when you lecture?"

I pointed to my home. Father was waiting outside, holding up the

52

blinds with one hand and peering out, his nose close to the window pane.

"Yes. That is a secret I wish you to keep, Margot."

He nodded his head toward my father and waited for me to enter through the door before leaving for his apartment.

"Good night." I whispered. Father locked the doors and asked about Mordechai. "He's not wearing the star, Margot."

"I know Daddy. Don't worry. He's a friend from the Zionist meeting."

Father kissed me goodnight on my forehead. And I am now dazed that Mordechai confided in me.

Perhaps he is not the only one who has feelings.

I recall that day in the park...the ping pong match....the beverage...

Let me read my favorite Dutch poems before I remember too much.

***

Where are all the Good Samaritans?

I had the misfortune of being an eye witness to a disastrous scene. An old lady with a Jewish star poorly sewn onto the back of her coat struggled to cross the main street. She seemed very old. Maybe eighty or ninety?

The sun was high, so it must have been noontime. She squinted as she crossed the road. All of a sudden, a Nazi guard's dog barked loudly in her direction. She became startled and then increasingly frightened (of his jaws, no doubt). Just as she continued to cross the street, a police car (with 'GS' written on it) violently blew her off the street and into the gutter. No one came to her aid. The car didn't even stop, and the guard standing near the entrance of the bank (where the incident occurred) did not bother to examine her. I was standing on the side the old lady wanted to reach. I saw everything, but I could do *nothing* to prevent it. How utterly helpless I felt!

I have little medical knowledge, but I quickly summoned an ambulance and began to check her breathing and vital signs. She appeared half-dead, but (thank God) she had only suffered a broken hip and dislocated shoulder. A Jewish volunteer from the hospital rushed her to the medical center. I believe she survived by pure miracle. I plan to visit her tomorrow evening. I don't even know her name, but I feel her sorrow. Her dentures were lost in the gutter at first, but I found them buried in refuse. I was looking for identification and instead I exhumed her 'pearls;' they were not very white. They were missing three teeth and some leaves were stuck to the palate. She lay mostly unconscious; she muttered some words. I could not make them out. I think she was praying *Shema Israel*, the prayer a Jew recites before death (if he's lucky enough to get the chance).

Why did the Nazi police car continue driving? Why didn't anyone stop and help the old lady? Whatever happened to the Good Samaritan? (How naïve, Margot!) I am so *scared* now. The Nazis have no respect for Jewish life. Can all those stories be true? If a person can utterly disregard the life of an old woman, a truly vulnerable citizen, what can be said for the stronger and more resilient? Do they even differentiate? Are we really like puffs of air or cockroaches? What are we to do as a nation? As a people?

How am I different from this old lady? I identify with her. I am her. The Nazi police car would have done the same to me were *I* the one who hesitated to cross the street. Before the invasion, the Amsterdam police and citizenship would never have permitted such a violation of human life! What's happened to the ordinary citizen? Have we lost the sense of responsibility for each other?

Anne asked me why I appeared so wan.

I didn't want to tell her the truth. I am utterly alone in my experience, it seems. If I told her, she would suffer just as I do now. I need to talk to *someone*, so I am writing in my journal. I don't know how much it's helping. But this is better than nothing.

***

I found the old lady from the car accident strapped to her hospital bed.

She has no name. She has a number, though. 149403.

She was, for the most part, incapable of communication. She lay motionless, unresponsive. Her mouth was wrinkled and curled into itself. Her dentures lay in a glass cup by the bedside table… (I made sure to give them to the medic yesterday.) They were a purplish color and magnified three times their size. I noticed another missing tooth.

She had some deep lacerations on her right cheek. Unlike a child with fatty cheeks, this old woman had no fat to protect her skin. She needed a couple of good stitches. I kept staring at her dentures. She needs new ones, I kept thinking. Maybe she couldn't afford them. How long has she had those wretched 'teeth'? How old *is* she? I couldn't ask her much.

Did the nurses find out her name? They were too busy tending to the flu victims, so I couldn't ask them either. For now, she is the Old Lady with Purple Dentures. Perhaps her children are worried about her? Perhaps her husband is still at home? What's to be done? (Does she even have a husband?) I do not recognize her from the neighborhood or from synagogue… I left the hospital room feeling completely inept and wholly sympathetic.

***

The birds and the bees: when babies swarm into the universe:

I went back to the hospital. I meant to visit the Old Lady, but I didn't get the chance. Yesterday, two nurses disappeared overnight, and the maternity ward is now short-staffed. As it turns out, *seven* women went into active labor roughly at the same time. Doctor Mann was rushing from one to the next—there were two women in some rooms— his brow accumulating sweat together with the screeching mothers.'

Doctor Mann yelled, "I need some help here!!"

Rika nudged me, so I quickly washed my hands again and ran to his side. Before I knew it, I was holding the thigh of a strange woman as the doctor began massaging the passage of the baby's skull.

"PUSH HARDER," he commanded.

The poor lady turned a dark-bluish color in the face; the baby did not budge. Doctor Mann exhorted me to explain how to push properly. I looked at him quizzically— I had no idea what to say! He read my expression very well and said, "From the abdomen, not from the face." (Ah… I thought. But I didn't let him know I was completely ignorant!)

"Push the baby using the pelvic floor muscles and your abdomen," I explained. "Don't hold your breath, but use your breath to push!" She nodded again and again in comprehension, and she pushed and pushed.

"Chin to your chest!" Rika came to my aid at this point. Doctor Mann bellowed again. He then instructed me, with gusto, to help by pressing my weight on her bloated belly. I followed every word he said. My hands were sweating as much as Dr. Mann's forehead and I was holding my breath together with the lady. (I later found out her name— Hanneke.)

Three more agonizing calls to 'push like you're making doo doo'; a pressing force on the abdomen (that would be me!); the mother pushing with half her head and half her abdomen; the impatient doctor massaging the poor woman's canal, exhorting 'harder harder!'; nurses pressing the doctor that another woman's baby is crowning; and finally!!! The hairy little baby squiggles through and out of his mother's womb. The baby's head was enormous! Hanneke was crying from relief. She held him immediately after she expelled the placenta. The mother fell silent as the newborn took center stage. Four babies were born. Three more were left.

Dr. Mann barely managed a smile before he was rushed to the lady next door (whose screams were by far the loudest and persistent) by her *husband*. His hair all disheveled, he didn't speak a word of Dutch. He pointed, fiercely, in his wife's direction and spittle sprayed the room. I believe he spoke in Polish. He probably said, "This woman has enough help. Go to my wife, she's dying of pain. The baby won't come out! Help us!"

Two nurses held him by the arms 'You're not allowed in this room, Mr....' 'You must leave immediately.' 'No men in the labor rooms— hospital policy—no exceptions.'

The husband shrugged them off. He grabbed Sophiia by the arm and led her to his wife. This was the woman whose baby was 'crowning' or just peeping through, but now his head was stuck inside her.

Dr. Mann began maneuvering the pelvis and the baby's head. He seemed to work very hard. He was laboring together with the woman, just without the pain. Two long, agonizing minutes later and another wail filled the room. The husband began dancing the hora around his wife's bed! He almost slipped on some of the surrounding tables and equipment, but he was too overcome to even notice. What joy! The papa held his newborn son in his arms as the mama wept. The papa handed the infant to his wife, and he began to kiss and hug Dr. Mann. "Dziękuję! Dziękuję!" He repeated. The new papa held the doctor's face in his hands as he thanked him.

Dr. Mann seemed surprised by the man's display of raw emotion; I don't think he's used to it at all, come to think of it. Sophiia extracted the papa from the doctor. Two more babies were yet to be born!

My job was to clean the rooms from the bloody remains of the day—the type of blood that is best to see, knowing life was brought forth into this world. Some women were still in tremendous pain, especially those who had given birth before. The mothers were at this point too exhausted to enjoy their babies—but we nurses and volunteers had all the pleasure of cooing at the tiny new people! By the end of the hour, four girls and three boys were born. I gave one cute boy my own nickname: turtle-boy. He was still curled in, like a fetus it seemed, even a couple of hours after birth. Sophiia tends to call all of the newborns 'birdies,' and Dr. Mann's forehead is finally sweat-free.

I believe I have finally discovered my life's mission—I am to follow in the footsteps of women before me and plunge into the mayhem of midwifery!

Tonight I feel I have been born again.

***

Mordechai left Amsterdam! He did not let anyone know of his plan to escape! I am in shock!

He left me this letter on our doorstep. I pasted the note into my journal, so I will have it for safekeeping.

> Dear Margot,
> You have been a faithful friend, and I valued your intelligent comments at our meetings. I enjoyed our intellectual spats, if one could call them that. I am privileged to have known you. I never met a girl who was as unaware of her grace and wit as you are. You are a beautiful soul. When I first saw you, I noticed a refinement reserved for princesses, and the more I spoke with you the more I gained a deep appreciation for you delicate and humble nature. Your inner strength shines when you smile. I hope you build a strong reserve, Margot, to withstand the upcoming storm.
> As you well know, I am committed to living out my

destiny in the Holy Land. I have made arrangements to leave Amsterdam for another location. I do not want to involve you, for your own safety, with sensitive information. Within a couple of months, with God's will, I shall arrive clandestinely at Akko, so as not to arouse the suspicion of the British naval guards. I won't be able to write for a long time, and I don't know what awaits you and your family. I pray I will one day meet you in the Land of our Forefathers.

Take good care of yourself, Margot! If not for your own sake, then for your family's. Never give in! Be strong—for you will need all the strength you can muster. God be with you. Shalom.

Mordechai

I can't believe he left! Mordechai is a man of his word. How it pains me now, to remember the way he last looked at me. That was the last time I saw him. It is no wonder he had worn that sad expression. How frightened he must be! How will he manage this escape? He most probably used his 'Herman' identity to leave Amsterdam's port. From there, he may sail to Africa or to some Mediterranean destination. Perhaps Morocco? He will sail past Italy, Greece, Turkey, Cyprus, and only *then* will he arrive in Palestine illegally in some dinghy. This must be an incredibly risky undertaking. To say the least. Maybe he has a rifle? He will need to protect himself from marauders or others. He said he was a quick learner. He will have to speak different languages to blend in…

I didn't realize up until this very moment, after reading his letter at least a dozen times, how much he meant to me. He gave me incredible hope and purpose in a time when all seems purposeless. He gave my life that ever-needed direction. I have him to thank, no one else. It was because of him that I finally realized that Palestine, nay, *Eretz Israel*, is my home and the country of my future. I will miss him— and I don't know if I ever will see him again— and that pains me more.

***

I am not sure what I should buy Anne for her birthday. Mummy and I discussed this over coffee and pancakes this morning. Anne loves to write, so Mummy decided to buy her a diary. Anne already chose the one she liked from the bookstore. We still have time, but in our family we like to be prepared in advance! I think I will buy her a fantasy or a literary adventure book. I am thinking I should introduce her to a history book perhaps. I hope that may excite her. She's turning thirteen, so she is officially a teenager. I hope she'll like my gift. I have to start saving from now. She'll receive a plethora of gifts; she always does. I won't be able to compete, but I know Anne will appreciate any gift I buy her, so that saves me unnecessary grief.

***

Late at night, often without my wanting, I think of Father's secret plans. Maybe Anne and I should have been on a dilapidated boat headed toward Haifa rather than in this house? Who knows what awaits us all. Maybe we would be safer in the placid waters of the Mediterranean than in this ever-threatening conquered land? Perhaps we should flee to England. I know we have family there. What if the war should last and last: how long will we be able to hide? How long can provisions possibly last? I fall asleep hoping Mordechai will, at the very least, have the chance of sailing toward Haifa—

And I. I can only dream of that chance.

***

Why can't I be more like Anne?

I have not written in my journal for a while. Anne's birthday came and passed uneventfully. She was probably the most excited girl in the neighborhood that morning. Her friends wrote her lovely birthday cards… she laughed…enjoyed her carefree moments. She was mildly excited about my gift, *Tales and Legends of the Netherlands* by Joseph Cohen. Anne keeps the mood up, with her joyful nature. She helps me keep a smile on my face, especially when she has one of her jokes to share. I should learn from Anne to be more positive!

I remember when Anne returned from school laughing and giggling, "Quack, quack." She walked around the house repeating "quack, quack" until she fell asleep. I asked her why she was so giddy. She then read her essay '"Quack, quack, quack," says Mrs. Natterbeak' ' with pride and gusto. Her math teacher Mr. Keptor insisted she write compositions to help cure her chatter. Anne says her composition convinced Keptor to overlook her in-class gossip, and now he laughs at the whole matter.

Anne is always surrounded by her many friends. Even when she gets into trouble she manages to charm her instructors! And I do believe she is gifted with the pen as well!

I often tell Anne that were she only to apply herself more diligently in her schoolwork, both in the sciences and in mathematics, she would surely succeed! She is social, to a fault, since her chattiness interferes with her scholastic aptitude. Perhaps it is better for her to remain the way she is, since, after all, I have come to bear witness to the benefits of good sociability and graciousness. Anne often appears sincerely animated and alive, 'happy' as it were. She especially comes to life around her 'boyfriends!' Lately, Hello Silberg has been coming around and asking for her. Mummy took a liking to him, since he is an attractive lad, "a decent boy." Anne plays the part of female wittiness and charm to perfection. She is both receiving of his opinions and gestures as well as mysteriously distant to Harry in certain ways.

I like to study the way she keeps what I call, "a bubble of protective space," when she is around these suitors of hers. It is as if she is curious enough about the male sex to engage in conversation, cycle around town, chit-chat idly, play backgammon and cards, but still child-like and uncomfortable with the yet undeveloped sensual side of her 'self.' I believe she may soon discover that many of these boys are interested in testing certain waters…

From my experience boys lose their innocence earlier than girls. I could be wrong, of course. In spite of it all, I know Anne is a beautiful soul (even if she is criticized quite a bit at times), friendly and sweet to anyone and everyone! (Except for truly annoying people…she's never rude, but I can't say in full honesty that she gets along happily with them either!).

I often compare myself to Anne, especially when I suffer indignities at school. It's not as if I don't have friends, I do. But I don't have as many people trying to be close to me or desperately trying to become my friend…

Anne once told me that I keep too many things inside— and I wonder if perhaps she does too, how else would she know?

She's right. Anne is smart in so many ways, but Mummy doesn't praise her enough for her cleverness. Instead, I am the "brilliant" one because I have excelled in the hardest courses in school and because my nose is *always* glued to some book. The only reason I love to read is because I gain insight into this very complex world.

I used to speak to Granny a lot before she passed on. She's the one who recommended Jane Austen and Charles Dickens. She read them in German when she was a young girl. We discussed Darcy and Eliza, Pip, the awful Estella, and others over biscuits and tea. She would soften the biscuits, dipping them into the tea, before she ate them, so she would have an easier time with her dentures. Her favorite novel is *Persuasion* and mine is *Pride and Prejudice*. We both agreed that Darcy the most gentlemanly and Captain Wentworth Austen's most romantic.

Without Granny's wisdom, I never would have realized that love is often a result of some type of growth engendered between two people, forged through self-awareness and forgiveness (at least in Austen's universe). Granny pointed out, for instance, how "Eliza begins to love Mr. Darcy after she becomes aware that her own prejudices against Darcy clouded the judgment of his character." She subsequently forgives his 'impertinent remarks' and realizes that she was insecure about her own family and had a hard time hearing her secret misgivings about her relations from a third party. Darcy's devotion to Eliza is therefore all the more incredible! Darcy becomes aware of the way he hurt Eliza and forgives her for the many 'indignities' he had to 'suffer.' Darcy thanks Eliza for making him truly aware of his shortcomings, and he thereby grows into a better individual. Their love was forged through courageous self-introspection, and of course, forgiveness for flaws inherently part of their personal makeup. In a way, each partner plays the "mother"— each directing the other how to make the most of him or herself. Through this connection, Granny pointed out, "Darcy and Eliza begin to merge as a couple in love."

She told me to be careful when choosing a spouse—not to be too picky about his appearance but to focus on his character instead. "Don't focus on what the eye can see, but what the mind can hear!" She warned me, though, to always feel "as though this is the only man in the universe

I want to go straight into bed with!" She was very funny! I reassured her I had yet to meet that type of man, and she winked at me! She warned me to "make something of yourself, don't live in your husband's shadow, but always remember your priorities begin with your family."

She liked to play backgammon with Anne, and she enjoyed a good joke. We listened to Beethoven and Shubert on the radio, and we liked to discuss which musician, Mozart or Beethoven, was superior. I insisted Beethoven, since he was deaf and had to compose despite his awesome handicap. Granny told me I am the child of modernity, and that no one can surpass the mathematical precision of Mozart, which places Mozart on the pedestal of perfection. We then came to a truce: both were geniuses, and we should not compare.

Granny would wait for me every afternoon, with warm pancakes and jam. She had the newspaper on the table, ready for me. She spoke in German and read the *Spiegel*. She would point and say, "Read this article here to me. The print is too small." She didn't want to feel as though she were bothering me or imposing, hence the yummy treat. Anne would listen half-heartedly, mostly licking her lips. She would kiss Granny on her bony cheek and say, "Granny! I love you! You're the best baker in all Amsterdam!"

Granny would praise Anne and listen to Anne's many stories with patience and amusement. When she died in 1942, Anne was immobile for two weeks. She lay in bed, quiet and altogether melancholy. Pim would try to console her. He succeeded for the most part, but she would quickly lapse into a pensive mood for days thereafter. Anne would draw pictures on blank sheets of paper, with messages for Granny, and fly the paper airplanes over the waterways as she sailed the Ferries. She chose different routes for each of her different messages. I went with her a couple of times; we cried together. This helped Anne find comfort I believe, but she hardly speaks of her sadness and her loss. One message was especially poignant, "You are alive in my dreams Granny. You are ever-present in my thoughts. I love you still." She wrote these words in a black fog; a ferryboat emitted the penned words. The boat was a brick-red, and the murky water concealed gray geese. There were little fish visible beneath the ferry and the faint hint of a hand waving goodbye in the horizon.

Anne could not remain saddened for too long. She was able to move on. Like Anne, I too had a hard time; but were it not for Anne, I don't know how well I would have dealt with my sorrow, since Granny meant a great deal to me too.

***

The Zionist meetings are a messy affair once again. I went half-heartedly yesterday, and to my grave disappointment the boys and girls were yelling at one another. "You dirty bastards!" "You incredibly pathetic idiots!" And so forth. It turns out one of the boys 'bumped' into 'by mistake' and 'accidentally' rubbed Sytie, the lovely Orthodox girl I met at the *Oneg Shabbos*, in a private area. The poor girl was crying, and a group of five or six girls were consoling her. The other girls, some I did not recognize, were yelling at the boys, since the culprit refused to admit to his offense; in the eyes of the girls, the boys assumed collective guilt.

Sytie was mortified, probably because he whispered something she didn't want to repeat. She attends an Orthodox school for girls in the basement of a rabbi's home. She is very modest and pure; she never touched a boy. "Why me? Did I do the wrong thing?" Her conscience burdened her with excessive self-judgment and guilt. I went up to her with a glass of water. "Sytie, you know it's not your fault. He was just testing to see how you would react to him." I pulled a chair and told her, "Sit down. Think clearly for a minute."

"I can't! When I first got my period my mother told me that a boy is forbidden to touch me. Ever since then I've been so careful around boys. My parents don't know that I'm here. But I was so good; I don't know why he did it."

"Who touched you, Sytie?" I prodded her.

Sytie seemed very irrational. "I don't want to let you or anyone else know—it will be evil slander." And so on. She guarded the boy's honor even though he disregarded hers. She refused to point fingers. The boys dispersed after the incident, and the new leader, Jakob Hirsh, took to the podium. By the time he started speaking Sytie and I left the room to the Ladies 'powder room' (a dingy closet with a small toilet and a dirty sink).

Sytie explained to me that, according to Rabbinic Law, a woman is *niddah* once she gets her period. That basically means that a man, married or not, is forbidden to touch her, hold her hand, kiss her, and of course! sleep with her. She said these laws are written in the Bible, which she referred to as the *Torah*. I explained to her that the law is not only meant for girls to obey and that in this case, the boy who touched her was wrong.

"But he probably doesn't know he's not supposed to," she said. Again, in his favor. She refused to blame him. I really wanted to know what he said to her, if he said anything at all to upset her so, but she wouldn't tell me due to her righteous nature.

"Are boys really crude like that?" Sytie asked.

"Some are. Some aren't." I answered.

"My father never spoke like that to anyone, I know it!" Sytie was intent on preserving the dignity of all the men she knew. I have a feeling she is a bit too innocent for her own good. She is seventeen. But perhaps that is not so bad, after all.

"When is a woman *not* forbidden to a man?" I asked.

"A married woman has to dip in the *mikvah* seven days after she stops menstruating."

"And then?"

"And then they can be together…"

I probably looked amazed and baffled because Sytie explained to me (in the 'office'; we had to leave the W.C. after five minutes, it smelled so bad…) that religious Jews follow the "Laws of Family Purity." She informed me that there are very old *mikvahs* all over Amsterdam, and that I probably have one near my neighborhood if I paid more attention.

The *mikvah* is an indoor pool of water, and the water must come from a natural water source. Here in Amsterdam that is not problematic at all since water is pumped from the nearby rivers into some of the indoor pools. A woman meticulously cleans her body and dips in the pool *naked*. She said the main *mikvah* of our city is beautiful and very-well kept. The water is constantly cleaned and maintained throughout the year, since the mikvah is open every night of the year besides for Yom Kippur Eve and the Eve of the Ninth of Av. (I asked her about the Ninth of Av in passing. She told me that the holy Temple in Jerusalem was destroyed that night and day, and sexual relations are prohibited.)

Her friend Lea married this past June, and Lea related these 'secrets' to Sytie. It turns out a *shidduch* is expected for Sytie as well, since she will turn eighteen in July. (A *shidduch* is an arranged meeting for marriageable men and women. The parents introduce the prospective couple and hope they fall in love. Something new I just discovered today—the way Orthodox Jews find their soul mates…) "But my parents are not sure this is such a good time to introduce me to a gentleman…" The war. I almost forgot.

A married couple practicing periodic abstinence! Who would have thought? Judaism is so very interesting, full of surprises really. I never would have dreamed of such a thing, but here it is: sexual relations are forbidden between a husband and wife so long as the woman menstruated and did not immerse in a pool of holy water after a period of clean, non-menstrual, days. Fascinating. I want to share this information with someone, just to hear what she thinks of it; I don't know what to make of this at all.

Dipping in holy waters— it all sounds very strange. Mystic. Otherworldly.

How could it be that I never noticed the *mikvah*? I will be on the lookout now!

Just a thought—isn't it very difficult to remain separated from a husband for an extended period of time?

At the same time, maybe this separation *helps* couples reignite their passion for one another?

I am very curious. Perhaps I will find a book on this subject in the library.

***

No more teachers…

Professor Kahn did not arrive in school this morning. Slowly, slowly, students and teachers are disappearing. (I would like to think they are on the way to the Holy Land, but who can afford to be delusional?) I'm deeply depressed from Mordechai's sudden disappearance. The Zionist meetings are no longer what they used to be. All I have are my prayer book and the 'Israel is your Home' booklet to remind me of better days. Moortje prowls the room whining; who would have thought a cat could be so perceptive? She's beginning to spend more and more time with Anne, since I have become a bore.

Mummy and Daddy are slowly hinting to Anne that her days in the

Stadstimmertuinen (our school is located there) will soon end. The news is taking time to sink in. He doesn't want Anne to feel too much trauma. She is anxious, though. This much is obvious to us all.

***

When the phone rings, my heart skips a beat!

I heard from Jetteke that the Nazis are beginning to make "house calls." They literally phone the home and ask for certain individuals to appear at a designated destination! I am worried stiff someone may call for Daddy or Mummy. Perhaps someone may even call for me because I clearly remember handing out my information to that ugly officer months back. If I think too much about this a sickening feeling will sink my stomach to my knees. I have a terrible premonition that we will get one of those dreadful calls. Any day now. I did not reveal my suspicion and fear to anyone, including Jetteke. I would share my worries with Mummy, but she has enough of her own.

On another note, Henriette confessed—she is no longer a virgin! She had to "rid herself of the burden" and she wanted to "live fully" because this war is a bad "omen for anyone." I did not have to overhear her this time. She declared her "freed status" as a "woman of the world" to the rest of the girls during Professor Kahn's non-class session. I had no idea she felt her chastity was weighing upon her like an incredible burden...

Most of the girls had a log of questions for her: did it hurt? Where did she manage to escape to? Who was the lucky gentleman? She didn't seem enthused but rather relieved or somehow less stressed. I think her behavior is bizarre. Who is crazy enough to risk a pregnancy during such precarious times? I hope she was boasting, and perhaps she was lying to gain the attention and favor of her friends. At this point, after some of the rumors I've heard, I am not surprised by stories of such immodesty. (I wonder what Sytie would say to this.) I've heard the Gestapo is especially brutal toward Jewish women. Some take women by force. Maybe Henriette wants to be in control of her own destiny? I will give her the benefit of the doubt either way. I pray this new craze is just another bad joke.

To get my mind off of things, I decided to look through my papers. For two full hours I made a list of what I wanted to learn during our indefinite "stay" in the warehouse. I also looked through old school notes and discarded nonessentials. Out went second form mathematics, first session biology, and many others. I retained Kahn's lectures, and I disposed of my less-than-amateurish sketches. (I have the bad habit of trying to draw people's profiles when boredom hits.)

Anne helped me, actually, so we chatted. She is beginning to become annoyed with some of her "beaus." Innocently, she asked me if I had a boyfriend. I told her I don't.

"Would you like to have a boyfriend, Margot?"

"Yes, Anne. I would. But I want a very serious man in my life, someone with whom I would be able to share all of my thoughts and dreams with," I answered. This answer surprised me. No one ever asked me that question. But now I guess the truth is out.

Anne then surprised me with a question, "Do you think Mummy and Daddy will get a divorce?" She had grave concern in her eyes.

"Why would you think such a thing?"

"Because they're arguing so much lately!"

I had to explain to Anne that Mummy and Daddy are arguing because they love one another, and us, their children. And this is the cause of their agony and anxiety.

"Do you think Hitler will win the war?"

Anne looked frightened. I wanted to lie to her and tell her that I knew for a fact that he would lose the war. But all I said was: "I do not know…I don't know…"

Anne will have to outgrow her childhood in ways I never had to. And just for that alone I will need to be patient with her. I hope I am strong enough for her to lean on.

***

Anne is beside herself!

Anne returned from school crying and in hysterics. One of her classmates was taken away. Mummy had to call Daddy from his office immediately to calm Anne. Her hands were shaking terribly and her lips parched from the profusion of tears. Anne couldn't stop repeating, "Will she die? Will she die?" over and over. Her tears did not subside for quite some time.

I never saw Anne like this before. Even when Granny died, I do not recall such hysterics, such immediacy. Anne is usually full of energy. It is hard to see Anne in frenzied panic. She is concerned, extraordinarily so, about this girl's well-being. One must admire her gracious spirit and generous heart. Mummy was unable to console her, and I was completely unaccustomed to such grief. I too felt at a loss. Daddy seemed to know how to speak to her, though (thank God).

"She will be with her family. They will look after her. Pray for her Anne, if you feel this will help." And so forth. Exhausted, Anne crawled into her bed with puffy, red-rimmed eyes and a tissue in her left hand to wipe her watery nose.

The sight of Anne's grief-stricken face haunted the remainder of the evening—and even in her sleep she seemed to weep some more.

***

The Lady with Purple Dentures (149403) disappeared. Her room is now occupied by a mother and child; both are suffering from a serious case of influenza. The child is frail, and the mother appears not much older than I. I introduced myself, but she did not stir. Her husband or father, I am not sure which, read the Book of Psalms by her bedside. He had side locks and a long, triangular beard. The beard was white, but his side locks were still tawny brown. His face did not appear too craggy or wrinkled with age, therefore my uncertainty. He did not take notice of me either.

I tried to gather information about the Old Lady, to no avail. The nurses said the Gestapo made their rounds yesterday, and the Old Lady was chosen for 'relocation.'

Sophiia is working double-shifts. Her eyes seem hooded now, and she is incredibly thin too. She needs as many volunteers as there are patients in the delivery rooms, but most women are either at home or afraid to leave their homes. I want to let her know that soon she will lose another volunteer, but Daddy said we are not to reveal our family secret to *anyone*. We cannot risk detection. The Gestapo instituted harsh laws against aiding Jews, so we cannot risk burdening people with information. Also, we don't know if we can trust anyone. That is a huge problem. Our neighbors may seem nice; they may say "hello" and smile, but who knows what they may do when the Gestapo threatens to blow their heads off in the middle of the night?

Dr. Mann is now working without some of his trusty nurses. He seems to age daily from the rigors of his workload. His wife left for Sweden; Dr. Mann refuses to leave his patients. Even during these hard times, life goes on, even with the constant threat of deportation. Life must happen just as death must. There is a delicate balance in this world, and Dr. Mann helps ensure that each child has the best possible chance for survival. Some mothers deliver their sons and daughters weeks too early; from fear and anxiety their uterus begins to contract and the baby is inevitably expelled. Dr. Mann must use whatever is at his disposal to support the neonate's frail body. One mother lost a son. I was not on duty that morning, but Sora, a middle-aged doula on call during the early morning hours, sadly reported the tragic incident. The baby was malnourished. The mother suffered from some type of thyroid disorder. I didn't catch all the details.

I worked alongside Steentje without saying much. Dr. Mann muttered in German, "Not enough supplies! Not enough gauze..." Steentje, a Dutch Gentile, thought he was uttering curses. I cleared the air between them. I translated his frustrations, and she seemed more at ease.

The post-partum mothers are no longer remaining for the recommended two-week period. It is unclear why this is the case. I suspect the strain on the families is too much during these difficult times. Sophiia says this is better for the maternity ward, since it is now even more short-staffed than before I began my volunteer work.

Just as I began feeling at home in the hospital I had to leave. My last shift was uneventful for the most part. Oddly enough, I recall nearly every moment. I was cataloging the day, the same way one savors a rich-chocolate desert after a brisk walk in late fall.

One mother, Rebeka Cohen, thanked me profusely for "all your help! You really made my time here in the hospital easier for me." Rebeka could not walk after delivering her nearly three kilo son. Petite to begin with, her son took after her husband, a heavy-set individual. I thought they made an odd couple, but they seemed to love one another very much. She labored for nearly four and a half hours, pushing, and pushing and pushing. Each time she felt a contraction and the fetus did not budge was like "a whirlwind of excruciating torture." (This is the best form of birth control—horror labor stories!) Her husband, Sophiia related, pulled his hair each time she screeched in agony. By the end of the four hours, he was nearly bald.

The child did not budge. (Dr. Mann made good use of his handkerchief, I can imagine!!) The doctor used forceps to dislodge the baby's head. After the shock of his delivery, Rebeka nearly fainted from fatigue. The nurses placed iced pads on her vaginal area to help reduce the inflammation and swelling. She needed many stitches (more than I'd like to think of). The nurses placed her on a gurney and rolled her into the postpartum rooms. She later confided, "I felt like a corpse. I was in so much pain I could not feel anything anymore." She groaned, "I want to die. I want to die." Over. Over. Over.

It was hard to see signs of suffering etched in her expression. Her eyes were soft, but weak, a certain vitality lost. When she needed to use the W.C. someone had to hold her up, propelling her forward. Her knees buckled from weakness, and her legs were often bloodied. She was embarrassed from her nakedness and her pubic hair. She tried to cover the area as she urinated. "It burns so much," she would whisper. Her stitches were far into the perineum, almost extending into the anus, so she winced when she passed gas. She "felt like a factory awfully damaged. I am reduced to my bodily functions." Worst of all, she needed to bathe after a couple of days with little respite from bleeding. Dr. Mann was worried about her and forbade her from walking at all. Using the bed "potties" was humiliating. Dejected, she would cry. Her baby boy, later known throughout the ward as Big Boy Abe, suckled whatever little was left of her. If she began to feel some respite from her hemorrhoids, her sore nipples, cracked and bleeding, gave cause for grave anguish. Her breasts were engorged at one point, and she barely had enough strength to manually pump the milk. Her son had a hearty appetite, so she did not need to resort to pumping after a week. Her regimen was 'stool softener' for breakfast and dinner. She did not have a bowel movement for more than a week! She said she "was more afraid of letting nature take its course than delivering another child." I can barely imagine the extent of her misery nor can I fathom the torment of her experience.

Rebeka needed help. She had no choice but to rely on someone. She was half a person. She wanted drugs to ease her into sleep, which she craved. After her prolonged stay in the hospital, Rebeka left, walking (if somewhat duck-like) with a beautiful and healthy boy. But she had paid a hefty price.

Women like Rebeka inspire me greatly. It was with great difficulty I said good-bye to the institution that harbored such incredibly courageous women.

Hopefully, the war will end before we know it, and I will return! Just as their pain eventually becomes a past-tense occurrence, so too "This shall end!" I know it will.

***

So they called for me after all.

Fear such as this I have never known. At first we thought the call up was for Daddy. When we later discovered that I was the chosen one, I nearly collapsed. Quickly, Mummy and Daddy called M.G... Loyal and swift, she took clothes with her, our textile provisions, to the Warehouse. I should be packing right now, but I can't focus on preparations. I am simply stricken with shock. We are not supposed to leave for another ten days! What's to be? Do they really take girls my age to concentration camps? When I heard stories in school or in the Zionist meetings, I felt somewhat protected from their fate. But now I am the potential victim, and suddenly the world does not appear the same. It is as if I am treading in very deep waters, waters I cannot stay afloat in without drowning in the process. I won't go to school tomorrow, and I won't play ping pong. I won't see a budding flower, and I won't hear motorcars whizzing by. I won't listen to Jakob's speeches, and I won't be visiting Dr. Mann's office or the postpartum women anymore. I won't feel the canal's wind. I won't bathe Gaby.

The Goslars! What will happen to them? They can't come into hiding with us. Gaby won't be able to remain quiet. She cries, and she can't possibly remain indoors *all day*, and for God knows how long!

Mrs. Goslar is pregnant. She is due to deliver very soon—how can she deliver a baby in hiding?

Oh! And to think that I won't say goodbye to Hanneli and Gaby. My heart aches.

Mummy and I feel tremendous sadness. We don't want to leave our adopted family behind, but there is no choice.

I should pack. But I don't know what to take. I will need clothes. Of course. But I will also need reading material to help pass the time.

And this diary. What should I do with this diary? Should I take it with me?

Mordechai won't know where to post letters. Will I be able to reach him?

I need to sleep but my mind won't let me.

I am too fidgety to write. And Anne is crying in the other room. I can't concentrate when I hear Anne cry.

***

The Warehouse—at the Back House. Prinsengracht 263, at Westermarkt. July 1942

The Prinsengracht canal is situated right near us, but we do not feel its breadth of freedom. Oddly enough it rained the morning we left our home for the Back House. I generally do not like the rain all too much, but I found the weather more in concert with my mood than I would have expected. I wore a ridiculous amount of clothes; I appeared a good ten kilos heavier than what I truly am. Anne was dressed for a winter storm, and I felt ready to jump into the canal from excessive heat.

Cycling was bittersweet. My last moments on the street were filled with fear. The beauty of the canal was nearly lost… Since I arrived earlier than the rest of the family, I had the chance to take in my new living quarters without any interference. I can't emphasize *enough* how disheartened I felt. Boxes were strewn on the floor and on the beds, rubbish in every corner; dust-filled closets, linens and bedclothes were piled nearly ceiling-high in the little room. The W.C. had a strange, musty smell, and to top it off, the kitchen floor was as dirty as a back street. I felt overwhelmed. I dropped my satchel on the bed, sat myself down in the corner and began to cry. I was miserable. Suddenly this incredible tiredness filled my bones, and I could not move. I lay motionless on the bed; I was useless that day.

Daddy and Anne took charge of the cleaning and organizing. I wanted to help, make myself useful, but I could not muster the strength. Anne and Daddy sewed 'curtains' that resembled a clown's quilt rather than anything else I can think of. They worked quickly and did not care if their work was sloppy. Mummy was barely capable of making use of herself as well. No one ate. I did not have an appetite. Daddy did not mutter a complaint. I fell asleep before five in the evening. I awoke the next morning with a terrible cold. I am still a bit ill, feverish and stuffy, but I felt this deep-seated need to write.

Last minute, I stuffed my diary into my satchel. It looks like a pocket-dictionary; it's quite small. I figured it will do me some good to write while we are away, on a sort of adventure in our hideaway…

I discovered this diary in one of the book stores off Utrechtsestraat. It came with a locket, in the shape of a Jewish star that opens and fits into the keyhole. Imagine a Jewish star locket that can open in two, placed face-down onto the front of the diary that with a delicate compression, unlocks the diary's secrets. (One has to open the squared casing on the front of the diary to reveal the star-like puzzle piece hidden inside.) I loved this feature and paid the full price with my birthday money. I write in the diary when oft I get into a pensive mood.

I wear the locket underneath my blouse, and I often feel it sitting safely between my breasts. I could not abandon the little luxury of sharing my thoughts with myself, expanding my ideas in the written form— one of the few hidden treasures that will always remain my own, even as the world becomes increasingly eager to take away whatever I believed to be 'mine.'

***

How much more codeine will I need?

I am exhorted by all, "Don't cough! The people next-door will hear!" Suppressing a cough when your throat is parched, scratched, irritated, and sore is a practice in self-control not even the Chinese have implemented in their notorious dens of torture. To lull me into silence, Mummy forces me to swallow codeine. I need large doses to get the all-too-necessary effect —the effect we all need for our safety. Mummy, just now in fact, asked how I'm feeling. Not too well at all.

Not too well at all…

***

A pet. A pot. And the Van Pels:

The Van Pels arrived and with them our Frankish ways have been placed aside. One must put himself aside when another enters the scene.

They arrived earlier than expected. The Germans are sending out house calls at an alarming rate. Papa and Mr. Van Pels have been planning this hideaway for some time now. Our families are good friends, and Mr. Van Pels is Pim's associate. There is a general feeling of responsibility and camaraderie between our families. I do feel, though, that Mummy would have preferred the Goslars.

Daddy is accommodating, and Mummy is trying her best to get along with Mrs. Van Pels, a histrionic woman greatly concerned with her appearance and overtly flirtatious with a man other than *Mr.*Van Pels. Peter, their son (he's about my age), seems oddly insecure and somewhat anti-social. He brought his 'darling Mouschi' (a cat) along. Of all things, Mrs. Van Pels brought a large potty! This potty must have cost her a pretty sum. It is painted a pretty pastel pink, and carnations added flair to the otherwise functional item. It was heavy, but Mrs. Van Pels did not complain about its weight, her indispensible potty a true necessity in the otherwise unromantic Warehouse. Mrs. Van Pels neatly placed the potty under her divan. She tended to this item before unpacking her other belongings. She brought hosiery, perfumes, lipsticks, nail color, magazines, and cookbooks with her, and she made sure to bring along a satchel of lingerie. She will not have evenings out, yet she brought high-heeled shoes. She will not attend the opera, yet she brought her satin opera gloves. She will need more than magazines to keep her busy, and half the recipes in those cookbooks of hers are useless. Who can find Brussels sprouts, shallots, mushrooms and sweet syrup during these wretched times? And most strange of all, she walks around in the evening with a fur cloak around her neck! And it is still summer!

Mr. Van Pels is a genial man and he seemed to take a liking to me. I recognize Peter from the secondary school, but he is just as mysterious to me now as he was then. He's awkward; he walks around with his back half bent, petting Mouschi's soft fur half the day. He doesn't speak to his parents much; when he does, they seem impatient with him. Mr. Van Pels is excessively strict with him, bossing him around when he sees fit, sometimes putting him down even when Peter is not around to defend himself. They treat him like a seven-year-old boy. Mummy and Daddy are entirely different people; Mummy complains about the Van Pels quietly to Pim. Pim tries to reassure her…

It is going to be a trial of character, this indefinite stay in our 'Back House Hideaway.'

***

I have not written in this diary for more than a month. Living in the Hideaway is tension-filled and boring all at the same time. I am becoming friendlier with Peter. He is not as strange as I once thought. He enjoys his carpentry, and he shows me some projects with pride. His father calls his hobby 'rubbish;' he wants Peter to become a professional, a dentist or an engineer. Father never once told me "Margot, you should do this or you should become that." And I'm glad, because who can suffer such pressures?

Speaking of indignities—bathing: a feat to accomplish. At first, I would wash in the W.C., but the room is too small; I can barely maneuver myself around the basin without zinging my elbow on the wall. And the room usually smells *awful*. We are forbidden to flush during the day hours. The walls have a permanent stench, no matter how much I scrub the bowl clean. How can I clean myself in there?

At first, Anne and I decided to bathe in the front office. We placed curtains and stood guard for each other. Once, Mr. Van Pels nearly walked in on Anne, but I stopped him just in time. I don't think his eyes would have made out much, since the room was half-lit. This incident made us both a bit uneasy. Upon Peter's recommendation, Anne switched to the large office W.C. I followed suit. It will have to do for now.

The Van Pels bicker and quarrel to no end. Mrs. Van Pels enjoys the drama of arguments, and she wishes to draw us all into her methods of madness. I do not involve myself whatsoever. Anne bears the brunt of Mrs. Van Pels's 'educational remarks,' and she suffers for every little 'misbehavior.' This is one of Mrs. Van Pels's ways of entering into arguments with Daddy and Mummy. Mummy does not heed Mrs. Van Pels, but she becomes riled, I can tell. It is not so very pleasant to have a judge and jury condemning your hard work every day; each time Mrs. Van Pels points out another fault in Anne she is ostensibly pointing fingers at Mummy and Daddy's 'failure' at parenthood. And what purpose does this serve? It is true Anne can be a bit spoiled at times, but she is the baby of the family, and she will outgrow this phase, just as any. It is hard enough to be an adolescent without the constraints we live in.

I read a book when things become tense. Speaking of which, I just remembered, the 'book' that sparked a near-out-war! The 'book' was none other than *Lady Chatterley's Lover*, by D. H. Lawrence. Mummy and Mrs. Van Pels decided the book was inappropriate for 'the children.' Anne and I were forbidden to read the book (she had little difficulty adhering to this rule!), but Peter's curiosity was piqued to no end, and he devoured every illicit word with ravenous hunger. He was caught once, but this did not deter him. While we were in the office listening to the radio, Peter was engrossed in the naughty book! His father caught him reading. Slap! Peter was severely punished for reading too much about the ways of men and women. I had not as of yet seen such anger in a grown man. Mr. Van Pels seemed ready to punch his son in the nose for disregarding his word. Peter taunted his father, "I'm not coming down!" Banished to the attic, Peter wanted the last say. Were it not for Daddy's wise counsel, Peter's nose would have been bent beyond recognition, I'm sure. For *three* days Peter did not speak to his family. For *three* entire days Peter and his father wore sour faces. Why couldn't they simply apologize, speak to one another, and move on? I felt as though I were intruding on some private family affair, and I did not like to bear witness to someone else's shame.

Sometimes at night, even late at night, I can hear Mr. Van Pels arguing with his wife. When Mummy and Daddy argue, they do so, but civilly. They do not bellow or call each other disgraceful names. ('Idiot', 'imbecile', 'dim-witted fool' are the ones I was able to make out.) The other night, I overheard Mr. Van Pels exhort his wife, "you are shaming us all with your flirtations! Who knows what they think of you! Stop embarrassing us!" She yelled at him, "If you paid more attention to me, I wouldn't start up with anyone." And he would retort, "No one can give you enough attention, you want too much! You self-centered woman!" In the morning, I tried as hard as possible to forget what I had heard, but I kept on hearing their arguments in my ears. In my imagination, I always thought men and women (married, of course) made love in their rooms; spoke kindly to one another, softly, endearingly. This is all very jarring for me. I can imagine that privacy is a difficult commodity in our times. I only hope that I won't fall into this terrible behavior when I marry. One always does learn from other people, good and bad, I suppose.

I am learning from Mrs. Van Pels *not* to be flirtatious. Especially with another woman's husband. Daddy does not even glance in her direction, but it is still hard to see him placed in such uncomfortable situations day after day. One would think she would gather that Pim is not interested in her, but no such understanding is in sight. At first it was the batting eyelash. Then, the priming of the hair. Up went the skirt; down went the front of her blouse (by a few centimeters) and of course, the constant chatter, "Don't you say so, Mr. Frank?" "Wouldn't you agree Mr. Frank?" "And what is your opinion on the matter, Mr. Frank?" These are cheap ruses to gain favor with Father. Mummy and I glance at one another knowingly. Father manages a pleasant but curt reply. Anne lip syncs the words silently behind Mrs. Van Pels sometimes, and this causes the Franks to laugh off the momentary discomfort. Thank Goodness for Anne!

Speaking of which, she is the object of Peter's new petting obsession. Mouschi was his target since the day we moved in, but lately he has been petting Anne, as if she were some pet. She should tell him to stop if she doesn't like it, because I have a strong feeling she doesn't!

Anne and I are not speaking much to one another these days. She tends to chat with Mrs. Van Pels, who is vividly responsive to everything she says. Mrs. Van Pels may be hard to put up with, but Anne seems to have taken a liking to conversations with her despite it all. There is some type of war going on between the two of them; they'll have to work it out if they are to get along in these cramped quarters.

***

We listen to the radio at night, and sometimes we hear information from Tel Aviv. It is then that I allow myself the luxury of thinking of all Mordechai said, all he warned us about. "The Germans will not stop at Stalingrad. They want world dominion. They will go to war wherever they deem it possible. They will spread terror and destruction; they will rule their conquered lands with the same brutality they have been keeping under their pillows for years now. As they gather forces to destroy all of Europe, they will keep their agenda clear to all—the Jew is the *supreme* enemy." He must have seen a great deal first-hand to have spoken that way.

It did not register as such, when I first heard him. I thought he was being 'prophetic' or Zionistic in some way.

Now it seems clear to me: he was speaking what we refused to hear all this time.

Intent on keeping things 'normal', we went to school, ate our Dutch pancakes, played ping pong and enjoyed biscuits and tea in the late afternoon. What a travesty it all seems now!

I would like to return to the idyllic life before the war, but that life was thinly veiled. So long as Nazis seek to destroy civilization and the Jews, a beacon of light, no life can be anything but a farce.

There are hardly any ways to resist the evil sweep of Nazism. The only way to combat the anti-human measures is to try and be as humane as possible. The battlefield begins in the hearts of all mankind. I hope I have the strength to overcome the hatred growing in my heart and focus my energies on helping those in need.

***

Margot Frank = designated dishwasher.

At first I felt washing all those dishes was a chore. Now I see it as a reprieve from all my reading and learning. I have been trying my best to keep up with school work. Daddy is assisting me at every corner. We read together, study English (one of my favorite subjects) and discuss the newest theories circulating in psychology, physiology, and even economics. Mr. K. lends us books. Anne has taking a liking to French, which grants me a 'school buddy.' We have instituted a book club. This week I'll be 'lecturing' on the first sections of *Paradise Lost*. I began reading the epic in English, but I had to look up every other word in the dictionary, and some words are not *in* the dictionary. (What does 'exculpate' mean?) I decided to simply read the work in translation for now.

Anne is quarrelling with Mother lately. Mother can barely handle Anne's "disregard." She feels estranged when Anne chooses Father's attention over hers. I try to comfort Mother. "Anne is an adolescent, Mother. She loves you dearly. Don't ever forget." As soon as Mother begins to cry, Anne follows suit.

Day by day we gather horrifying pieces of information. Sytie and her family, as well as a dozen others, have been loaded into cattle cars, headed to Westerbork. The detention camp for refugees is now a resting stop for Holland's Jews. M.G. described the living quarters as "a camp for breeding illegitimate children." Do the men, women, and children share bathrooms, living space, and bed quarters? I can only imagine what goes on there! There is no privacy. People, without their wanting to, become voyeurs and worse. It is hard enough to maintain privacy and dignity here, in our Hideaway—how much more so in Westerbork? I cannot complain! I haven't the right!

That is not the worst, not at all. It seems, for Jews, situations go from worse to even more so. After remaining in Westerbork, under these preposterous 'accommodations,' Jews are shipped once again to Eastern Europe. The BBC news spokesperson said, "These human shipments are offloaded to secret locations and gassed by lethal chemicals. The remains of the Jewish bodies are then buried en masse." Anne and I gasped. Mother covered her hand with her mouth. Mrs. Van Pels nearly collapsed. Father's brows furrowed with deep worry, and Peter left the room.

I have a hard time imagining such a death. Choking on toxic air—why this is the way vermin are exterminated! Our school was fumigated a couple of times, and each time we rid the building of pests Anne and I did not attend school for days at a time. When we returned we still smelled the awful remains of the chemicals in the air. I walked around the building with my inner elbow covering half my face the entire day! I would strategically sit near a window and gasp for clean air whenever I felt nauseous. We opened the windows, even though it was chilly out. Anything for air.

What is it like? Choking on the fumes and the toxic buildup of gases in your own body? With so many people sharing your fate. In a large room. Without the chance of escaping your death: who would have thought a person could become an entrapped cockroach?

The Nazis wish to fumigate Europe of all Jewish vermin.

This is a slow death, surely. A cruel death, certainly. I haven't the head to contemplate this further. My head is beginning to ache, and my chest is tightening. I am taking deep gulps of air, as I write.

I don't want to die like this! Please God in Heaven! If I am to die, as we must all one day, let me die in my sleep; let me die with air in my lungs!

***

I let Anne read parts of my diary. In return, she let me read parts of hers. I let her read the first couple of pages, 'safe' entries! The rest is still very private. We came to this 'deal' on a Thursday evening, last week or so. Anne has become friendlier ever since our studies together. I am very grateful for this, since I have been feeling lonely lately.

She climbed into my bed, and we began chatting. Half the time Anne was kicking me with her knees, but I didn't mind much—I was too busy trying to come up with answers to her questions.

"Margot, can I read your diary?"

"Margot, do you know what you want to do after the war?"

"Margot, will you remain in Amsterdam and work here?"

"Will you marry after the war?"

"Margot, do you think I should become a journalist?"

"Margot, am I so very ugly?"

I tried to evade most of her questions, especially about my future profession. I'm not ready to let Anne know! And I love to keep my secrets, of course! I thought it strange, however, that Anne considered herself, in a remote possibility, 'very ugly.' Anne needs to know that she is *not* ugly, not at all.

"Anne, you are quite attractive. And you have nice eyes…" I don't suppose she was satisfied with this answer, but that is all I said. Perhaps I should have elaborated. "You have a friendly disposition. Most boys seek your attention. You are witty. You have very nice brows, a clear complexion, big, round eyes, delicate hands, a charming smile, a gentle mouth, rosy cheeks, beautiful nail beds," and so on. Anne needs a great deal of praise; she thrives on it! Before our escape, Anne received attentions from many boys and girls—this helped her self-esteem tremendously. Here in the attic, she is alone, with herself to study and her looks to critique, her personality to criticize (along with Mrs. Van Pels) and her life to analyze. I know this because I sometimes fall into a similar trap! We teenagers all, at one point, suffer from too much introspection!

Peter studies with Father, and I join them. Anne is trying to catch up, so she can join us. This will be very hard for her. Father is encouraging, though.

Anne can become edgy, which places us Franks in uncomfortable situations. I have my moods too, which I have such a hard time overcoming,

God knows! There is a tug of war between Mummy, Daddy and Anne of late. Somehow, I get mixed in too. Everyone is on edge here, and we are getting on each other's nerves.

Mummy is a darling. She listens to my complaints patiently. Father's calm comportment is a source of strength. He takes responsibility for us all and reassures me all the time. Father always had to work hard to achieve success in life. I think this has made him exceedingly resilient. I wish resiliency was viscous and could rub off on someone else, like sticky glue. Then, it wouldn't be so hard to be brave.

***

Peter has been chatting with me lately. He is quiet, most of the time, but he has opinions of his own, just like everyone else. It is sad to note, but Peter is quite insecure. The only child has to bear the brunt of it all: the hopes, aspirations, faults, and failures of his parents. And all alone. He is his mother's pet on good days, his father's punching bag on bad days, a silent ghost on others. He has taken a liking to Daddy and spends more time with him than with his own father. Mr. Van Pels is a good man, but he is ill-tempered to a fault.

We all have our Achilles heel it seems. Our 'fatal flaws' do serve us ill! I did begin to notice how children all too often reflect their parents' shortcomings, and the child with the greatest shortcomings becomes the oft berated child. I imagine in every family there is at least one child who becomes the 'incorrigible one.' The child begins to feel that indeed his essence is such and begins to behave incorrigibly, thus completing a self-fulfilling prophesy. That is too bad.

In our family, it seems, Anne bears the brunt of 'Frankish imperfection'—but she is not any more imperfect than I. Yet she believes she is alone. Perhaps we can help her by letting her see that indeed no one is perfect; we all have faults. Some of us are just better at hiding them! Anne is berated, mostly for silly 'wrongdoings.' The adults and the children are very edgy, but there is little to help diffuse the tension. Usually, Anne simply needs to stroll outdoors or to have a nice break from the rest of the family.

In general, it is very difficult to swallow criticism. I have an extraordinarily hard time with criticism; that reason alone is enough for me to try my utmost to behave exceedingly well. That is not to say that I do not falter. King David, the messiah, the Prince, faltered before the Lord. And he rose. Although we are all far from their greatness, we can certainly direct our eyes toward their stalwart ways and gather strength…

Gathering strength is perhaps the only treasure one may find within himself—and become a wealthy man in the process.

Anne shared with me a couple of her diary entries. She ran to her room excitedly to fetch her red checkerboard diary. She speaks to her diary as if she were a shadow of some kind. She calls her "Kitty". She writes to her like the truest friend. Her diary will be like one extended letter to a distant friend! Anne says "Kitty understands her completely." Poor Anne! She feels she is held to a standard of some kind. She is held to judgment… She feels surprisingly misunderstood, and she tries so much to communicate all the time! Hence the imaginary friend. How brilliant! I never thought of writing in my journal in the same way!

***

I have been praying from Daddy's prayer book lately. He reads in German, and I try to practice my Hebrew alongside the German, but it is so very hard to study a Semitic language without proper instruction. The Hebrew lessons of my youth have helped me, but only on an elementary level.

I have taken a strong liking to Psalm twenty-three. I committed the words to memory. These words may have been written millennia ago, but they resonate today, and particularly within our own lives.

"The Lord is my Shepherd! I shall not want." God indeed watches over us. He makes sure we are not consumed with hunger. "He leads me beside quiet waters."

Our Back House is near the canal; when I feel especially depressed at night, I fall into a deep slumber and awake refreshed and more hopeful. God has restored my soul.

Beneath us, on Prinsengracht, women and children are gathered into Gestapo headquarters, marched into trains, deported to Westerbork… Our Warehouse is in the Valley of Death, yet we tread upstairs peacefully, our stomachs full and our beds waiting for us, warm to the touch. King David and I share the same sentiment: "Even if I shall tread through the valley of the shadow of death, I will not fear evil—for You are with me." When I hear the thunder in the late evening and I see bolts of lightning in the sky I remember there is a Lord who created the Heavens. And He is above feeble humans. "Your rod and Your staff—these shall comfort me." As the Gestapo hunts for Jews down below, I prepare the evening meal with Mummy. As the trains fill up with unfortunate mothers suckling their babes, my pitcher flows with water and my bowl steams with warm broth. "In the presence of my enemies" God has "prepared a table before me," and my "cup overflows." Even when I fear the worst, I pray that God holds a place for me near his Heavenly throne. And as I hope for the best, I pray I will have the courage to live a renewed life of love for God and His people in Palestine. "Surely goodness and love will follow me" if I follow the dictates of the Lord. And if "all the days of my life" shall be many here on Earth, I will be gladdened by my good fortune. But if my days shall come to an abrupt end, I pray "I shall dwell in the house of the Lord for all eternity."

***

Love— among the ruins?

I've been thinking of Mordechai of late. I asked M.G. to secretly check our mail, but she said this would arouse the suspicions of the Gestapo. (*M.G. is none other than our heroine. Beep and Mr. K. are our guardian angels. Anne pointed out that I should protect the Van Pels too, but we are together in hiding, so I don't see a point in that.)

The Jews are incapable of escape, it seems. Mr. Pfeffer, our new compatriot in hiding, (who, by the way, is sharing a room with poor Anne), revealed pieces of information we would have been happier to do without. "Ignorance is bliss." But we owe our fellow Jews some compassion, even if it is in the form of tears. The brutal Nazis knock down doors with lists of 'Jewish vermin' for transport. Women are shoved out of their homes, expectant mothers and postpartum ones with newborns, old men and women, without coats, boots, or scarves, into the frigid streets. Truncheons in hand, they strike anyone who fails to comply.

Mr. Pfeffer relayed a terrible story: his niece was in hiding but had to see a doctor. She was pregnant, and she fell ill. Her family did not want to send her out of the house for fear of discovery. Later that night, she lost consciousness. Her mother feared the worst and ran to the hospital begging for a doctor to call on her daughter. Someone must have leaked information, and now they are all on some train bound for no-man's land. Their fate is left for us all to imagine. Anne could not bear the story; she summarily ran to her room. She most probably wrote an entry in her diary. She has the habit of writing when agitated. God knows she has what to write. (As no doubt do I.)

I wonder what has become of Mordechai's family. His sisters and mother were stationed in Westerbork for a long time now. Were they shipped off? And where is he? I would love to think of him safely sipping a cool drink in the heat of the Mediterranean desert. The sweat on his brow as he slowly cools his throat is a tantalizing image in my mind's eye. I hate to admit my weakness or reveal my secret soul, but I do feel a gravitational pull toward Mordechai. I have been denying my emotions from the start. I cannot bear the thought of knowing another person can have such sway, such incredible power over me! I am too proud for my own good!

It is a wonder how much yearning a young woman can carry in her heart for a gentleman's embrace. I feel my cheeks rosy up… the longer I remain confined in the Back House, the longer I desire to sprint across mountains…and trail valleys… To busy my restless mind, I stare at beautiful artwork and picture books. I let my mind flow with wonderful visions of romance… some too private to commit to paper.

As death looms, I feel drawn to life. But I have no hope of fulfilling wishful dreams here, in this padlocked home, in the heart of a battlefield.

***

Frank sisters once more!

Anne let me read *another* portion from her diary today. She shares with Kitty many of her personal thoughts, as do I. She has a hard time getting along with her roommate, Mr. Pfeffer. She calls him "Mr. Dussel," which means "idiot". He is not used to the company of children… Since I am a woman by every measure, I could not continue to sleep in the same room as the dentist. Anne, Mummy and Daddy decided, is still a young girl. We shared a room at first, but once Mr. Pfeffer came into hiding I had to leave. Poor Anne! She's slowly becoming a young lady, and she shares a room with a grown man!

I now sleep near Mummy and Daddy. It is awkward too. It is unnatural to share a room with one's parents!

She became the inevitable roommate… Anne and "Mr. Dussel" don't get along at all! She writes about his strange habits in her diary… The dentist suspects as much. Anne doesn't really care because writing to Kitty at this point is her only outlet.

Her loneliness is not disregarded or ignored. She probably feels the same way I do, but she reacts differently…It was good to read her thoughts, though. Kitty makes a patient friend, which she needs very much right now.

We Frank sisters are more alike than we would care to admit. Hence our diaries!

On another matter: the Frank sisters have become spies of the Canal street. We don't want to admit it, but we watch the men and women on the street and across the canal with too much interest. I am a bit ashamed of this sport, but we cannot help ourselves. We watch the street below before and sometimes after our baths. How much can we study, read, fuss about the house, scratch old stains, and peel half-rotten potatoes? We need entertainment! Our theatre has become the street. Our feature film never repeats itself. We have ongoing, streaming bits of reel at any moment we desire! It is simply perfect.

The "actresses" are neither skinny nor beautiful. Indeed, many are plump and avocado-shaped. The bargeman immediately opposite is now known as "Cornelius the Budge-man," since he is always shifting loads around the deck and yard. His noisy pet dog I call the "Boo-doo" since he likes to answer nature's call in hiding spots. Anne likes to refer to his wife as Bloedworst, or Blood Sausage: the woman's flaming red hair tops her oblong figure, and from far she looks like a packed sausage, especially when she wears her red dress. She seems unkind, and we catch her spanking her son, also red-haired and robust, with a wooden ladle. Creative humor can now take a front seat: Bloedworst Mother chases her son. Son, all too-churlish, begins to empty mussels back to their homeland, the Zeeland. Boo-doo joins the mess. All this happens as Mr. Budge-man is on the street trying to sell yesterday's catch. Someone points to Son, and Cornelius becomes Cornelius the Red. His anger is palpable, and Churlish Son runs squealing into the house. Commotion soon ensues, and Son is banished from sight. Mother Sausage rushes to the street to continue where her husband left off. The crowd begins to disperse as the Gestapo come on the scene and ruin our few moments of entertainment, filling us all with terror.

Sometimes, a reprieve is only that— a reprieve; Anne and I move away from the window, go back to the Hideaway and help Mummy peel potatoes. Perhaps we have been too silly for one day.

***

I am noticing that my mood shifts from month to month. A couple of days before I menstruate I feel my mood drift into very shallow waters. I am very short-tempered then. In order to avoid becoming a nuisance, I work on some advanced mathematics. When I tire, I begin French. The subjunctive. The present tense. And so forth. When I grow bored of this, I locate the book cards and begin a short synopsis of the book I last read. And I must whisper if I wish to speak. We whisper all the time here during the day. Sometimes, I think I hear Mr. Pfeffer whisper at night Shh!! To his young companion in bunking. We are overwrought with fear (even when we should have some respite from that fear). When I feel consumed with writing, I climb the stairs and have a short chat with Peter. Sometimes he helps me 'build' an interesting 'piece of furniture,' one of his handy additions to our drab house. I asked him about the Zionist meetings, but he said he had never attended. When he asked me *why* I was curious, I did not offer a clear response. I shrugged and moved on to another subject.

There are too many awkward silences lately. Conversation barely flows. Sometimes I sense that he just wants to be alone, so I go back downstairs. By this time I am ready to help Mummy with dinner preparations. My domestic duties take over: I dust the ever-dirty pantry and scrub some dishes that always seem to have some sort of residue. To be honest, I become disgusted from the dirt to the extent that I lose my appetite. We do not have enough cleaning products to properly maintain hygiene. This is a source of unwelcome unpleasantness. Our rations decrease as the war protracts. And we are becoming accustomed to lower standards of cleanliness...

We eat beans many times a week, and they are *dried* beans. The house shakes and tumbles at night—and not from an air raid! In every corner one can hear the evenness of quiet repose, and then an explosion from the North! From the South! Eruptions spur the Back House Hideaway: invisible gaseous ruptures fill our nostrils with toxic fumes… and the space between us all is erased, by the indestructible power of the bean!

I laugh now, as I write. Mrs. Van Pels wants to know why I am giggling. I cannot let her know that her secret is out, as is mine, Anne's etc. She thinks I am writing something derogatory about her! "Is it about me?" Even though I am writing in a relatively quiet corner of the house, Mrs. Van Pels managed to peep into the room and witness the all too revealing giggle. "Don't worry Mrs. Van Pels." I told her. "I am recalling an interesting episode of my youth." Mrs. Van Pels cocked her head and nodded. "Darling, then, have a good laugh. So may it last."

The bean is not our sole enemy. It seems the pea and the half-rotten potatoes are runners-up. Just the other day Mrs. Van Pels had to make use of her pastel potty *twice*, and all that *before* noon. I am beginning to prefer eating small pieces of bread, and if that is not available, dry biscuits. If I must, I consume bean dishes *as little as possible*. I hope no one takes notice, but this is bound to become an issue; all behaviors are monitored *at all times* in our escape house by nosy personnel. Thankfully, Mummy does not prod, and she has stood up for me in the past. I am too tired to become my own lawyer. One must preserve one's energies for controlling nostrils from unwelcome unpleasantness!

***

Chanukah came and went. We did not celebrate the holiday in the way I would have liked. The Festival of Lights. When I think of the large torch we lit back at our secondary school yard in commemoration, I begin to lose my sense of reason. I hate crying. Perhaps I will allow a tear to flow. Perhaps I should be festive and allow eight tears, one for each night of the Miracle of Light… I am in a pensive mood, that is for certain! And sarcasm does not suit me well. So. I will begin again.

Chanukah came and went. I love this particular holiday. Mordechai spoke of the Hasmoneans a great deal. "The Maccabees were not afraid to revolt against Antioch! They raised their swords to the Heavens and demanded, 'He who is with the Lord come forth and follow!' A group of renegades, untrained yet undaunted, combated and defeated the Elephant-led Greeks." They should not have been able to defeat them, but the Lord delivered the Greeks into the hands of Judah and his fearless brothers. This endurance was a sign from the Lord of Israel that He was with them during their battles; indeed, He battled and He marched His children into victory.

But the Temple on Mount Moriah was defiled by the pagan Greeks. They sacrificed swine on the altars of gold and copper, the most impure of all beasts, according to Jewish belief. God delivered the Jews, but they were robbed of their ability to communicate their gratitude to the Lord and to fulfill their duties as priests of the Holy Temple of Jerusalem. In an act of solidarity with His people, the Lord blessed the anointed and untainted oil (a single flask contained this oil. It was the only one found with the Seal of the High Priest, the mark of purity) with the magical ability to burn for eight full days (until another virgin olive oil flask could be arranged for), even though the small canister of oil would not have sufficed for more than one day.

According to Jewish belief, the Lord assists those who make an effort to fulfill His commandments. Mordechai explained some of this to me, and the rest I read in the long *Tenets of Jewish Philosophy*.

I wonder if fulfilling commandments in a time of war is doubly rewarded. How we can use salvation now!

Perhaps M.G., Mr. K. and Beep are *our* saviors? They climb the stairway, past the revolving bookcase, and share with us books, the news, even day-to-day matters with good spirits. I look forward to their visits; it is as if I am like an old lady in a nursing home awaiting my relatives…some human contact… How we crave the outdoors! I smell the cold weather in M.G.'s coat. I feel the streets in their shoes, when they walk by me.

I crave the outdoors. The beauty of a rose remains for others to inhale.

How I would love a miracle!

This year, I wonder if a miracle will transpire for the descendants of these brave Hasmonean princes. Perhaps God will fight our war against the barbaric Germans; certainly they destroyed enough synagogues in all of Europe to earn the comparison with the Greeks, who defiled the Great

Temple of Jerusalem with marble statues of Athena and Apollo, brazenly naked and silent.

It amazes me—I was not alive during that wondrous time in Jewish history, yet I identify with the people of that era as though I were a part of the story itself!

Perhaps I am a reincarnation of a Judean Princess? How romantic to contemplate!

Jewish mysticism points out that reincarnation is indeed a "true" reality. Different religions believe this as well.

Who knows?! Perhaps after the war I'll send a question to a scholarly rabbi…

The story I love best of all—now that I am on the topic of Chanukah—is Judith and Holofernes! A beautiful Jewish widow, her husband slain by brutal Greek warriors, seeks revenge for *all* Jewish widows. Unafraid of the great Greek general, she brilliantly makes use of her awesome beauty to lure Holofernes into a fatal moment of weakness: she leisurely feeds him heavy cheeses and strokes his mighty thigh as she pours wine down his thick throat. She lazily pats his brows and combs his beard with her long fingers to calm and soothe him. When he is lulled into a drunken stupor, she pulls a sword and slashes his ugly neck. *Decapitated*, Holofernes is now forever *incapacitated*! Judith raises his gory head by its long strands of hair, sticks it onto the sword, hoists her spoils of war and exits the tent. The soldiers gasp in utter horror and flee the encampment! How does a woman gather such strength? She did not need to lift her voice nor fight her way through dangerous terrain. She simply honed her gift of beauty to encourage the women of Israel and the people of her nation to unite in the spirit of resistance and defiance.

I do not feel that gathered storm of defiance has enjoyed such success today. This is unfortunate. Sabotage *is* common. Thank God the Dutch are organizing clandestinely. The Underground is active; we hear stories of German offices suddenly blown apart… these are good signs for us all. However, it is not enough. Transports and arrests are daily occurrences. The bombings and air raids are increasing in number; the war is carrying on and on…

The electricity is out again. I must wait for another day to continue.

***

I hope no one will ever read what I am about to write. I dreamed of Mordechai, and I awoke with pangs of longing. Such longing. Dreaming. Vivid and clear; disappointingly unreal. So strange; I've never known such desire…

Mordechai stands, in the Judean desert, as I lay nearly motionless on the desiccated branches of an acacia. He supports my neck, holds my back tightly with one arm. In his other hand he holds a crisp and penetrating cup of water. He raises my head and begins to pour the drink slowly, patiently, down my throat. My eyes peacefully rest on his. And his on mine. Slowly, my hair begins to swirl, unremittingly; a dust storm gathers…The waves of sand engulf us. We are blinded. But we are locked in a primordial embrace, holding each other close, and we are protected. The gusts now settle, Mordechai lifts the chalice. It is empty of its nourishing waters.

And in its stead—grains of sand. Mordechai holds me tighter, and I awake. A throb. A pang.

Of unquenchable desire.

I am plagued by my craving to embrace him

And by ever-constant fear of death by thirst.

A terrible feeling of paralysis grips me just as I am overwhelmed with bliss…

I close my eyes again. I try to recall my dream, the sensation of cool waters tunneling down my throat… I cannot regain the memory; the senses fail me, even with time stretched out before me in seemingly endless waves.

As our lives become harder to bear, I am drawn more and more to whimsical visions. But these fantasies contain elements of fear;

Fear I cannot escape, even when I dream.

***

Good news is tempered with bad: the Allies are slowly encroaching on enemy terrain, but the Germans remain embroiled in the blood bath they have drawn; the rags are soaked and the ground is saturated with Jewish blood.

Air raids are a constant threat; our slumber is disturbed almost nightly. I think longingly of the new mothers back in the maternity ward. (I wonder if Dr. Mann and Sophiia are still working there; many professionals are still in Amsterdam according to M.G.) I have a hard time concentrating on my readings during the day, and Anne and I often chatter to keep up the morale.

The air raids are a personality-revealer:

Mrs. Van Pels reacts with sheer hysteria. Her husband wishes to continue his snooze, but his wife robs him of that chance.

Peter is stunned as he is silent. Father is reassuring and supportive. Mummy is fearful, but she leans on Father for support. The grayish dentist is nervous and rattled. Anne is frightened, concerned, and overtly in need of calming. I am frightened, outwardly composed while inwardly shaken.

And that leaves Mouschi-the cat-inured to the noise. Roaming around, she searches for dinner.

I noticed cats can go for days without much to eat. Let me not mention the rats. Humans, the greatest of all God's creations, are by far the weakest. They have tried to assume greatness in so many different realms. And they *have* achieved. A great deal. Yet we remain frail. Humanity has much to gain from remembering this humbling fact. But for all the strengths of the human mind, humans remain the most forgetful…

The air raids torment us all. It is as if we are destined to fear our deaths time and time again. I have a hard time falling asleep once the raids subside. My heartbeats echo in my ears. My blood vessels pump and pump—loudly. I am sleep deprived and my head is heavy—another price we must pay.

***

Our house on Merwedeplein was so lovely; now look at us! It is funny to think how only last year we celebrated Anne's birthday amidst gifts and abundance. This year Father and I worked on a poem to commemorate her birth date. She will have to find solace in our respect and understanding, our love and our desire to put a smile on her face. This is all we can offer. Father composed a poem for me on my birthday as well. Mummy hugged me and Anne kissed my cheeks. It was sweet. And it was enough. At times like this having loved ones close to you may be the greatest gift of all.

***

Anne and I file papers for B., write in the sales book, and type letters of correspondence. She often requests our help, and we are more than glad to oblige. Funny to think how one may see such drab work as completely uninteresting, even boring. But we enjoy our work—since our day-to-day lives are monotonous, and our hours filled with all-too-similar routines. What once was white is now black, and what was black is now white. Just a thought.

***

Break-in!

Anne and I are speculating as to who may have broken into the warehouse! Hoodlums, certainly, but are they potentially dangerous to our hideaway? On and on we debated this topic, until exhaustion overwhelmed our senses.

When the burglars caused such uproar, the palpable fear on everyone's face gave me pause. What if we were discovered? What would become of us? I needed to use the lavatory badly after this episode. But father insisted that I "hold it in." I cannot describe how painful it was. I had no choice—I had to beg Mrs. Van Pels. Father was kind enough to ask for me. Thanks to Her Royal Potty, I was somewhat able to regain my composure. Our bodies become our very own prison sometimes! Certain functions of the human body are simply out of our control. This is unnerving! And humbling.

How I want to take a warm bath after such indignities! But I must wait. I share this with you, my locket-diary; for, whom else would I trust with my private thoughts? On private 'functional' matters no less!

I guess I can laugh it off now that the stressful moment has passed.

***

Bullets fly overhead. Yet we are protected by Providence. Of this I am certain. More than once I held unto the banister by the stairs, knees bent, praying for bombs to freeze in midair, to land far away from our home, far away from me. I have witnessed paratroopers die, landing in the blazing canal, their parachutes unopened. I have seen bombs in midair, headed straight for our neighbors, and detonate farther south. I have heard the air raid siren countless times, and each time my feet buckle. I am standing on a precipice, and what holds me upright? The Lord of the Mighty and the

Weak. I begin to chant Psalm 23. I close my eyes and imagine the halcyon days of my early youth.

The sky, ablaze with dusty embers, glazes the darkness. Anne whimpers in Daddy's bed; we are all afraid to die.

And I, too big to climb into bed with Mummy and Daddy, clutch tightly the prayer book Father has kindly given over to my safekeeping. I open to any chapter of King David's supplications and read the words, slowly, deliberately. Often, the book opens to Psalm 27:

The Lord strengthens me—whom then shall I fear? "Though an army besieges me, my heart will not fear."

Tears drop onto the yellow-torn pages, upsetting the dye. When I pray "though war break against me, even then will I be confident," my throat threatens to choke the very breath from me. I don't want to wail. I don't want to succumb to my overwhelming trepidation. Loudly, with my voice in my ear, I recite, "He will hide me in the shelter of His tabernacle and set me high upon a rock."

I then realize our position may be vulnerable, but our hideaway may also serve as our very protection. Unaccustomed to ongoing conversation with the Lord, I beseech, "Hear my voice when I call, O Lord; be merciful to me and answer me!" Sometimes, the bombs become loudest at this time and I must stop reading and run to another room. My faith is tested, my resolve— a question of survival. I have no choice but to seek the Lord. And I do. "Do not forsake me!" My God, I realize, is my Savior. The tide within my soul begins to turn, and I anxiously seek inner peace. If I die, I tell myself over and over, if I die, I will seek goodness in Heaven. I will strive to be close to my Maker. Confident in His Mercy, I silently pray, "I am confident…I will see the goodness of the Lord in the land of the living." Either today, tomorrow, or when I am old and gray from surviving this wretched world, I will "wait for the Lord;" I will "be strong and take heart. And I will not despair the Lord."

And in this way I gather strength from an ancient text at a time when such a text mocks the regime of the anti-Jewish crusaders.

***

M.G. has managed an incredible feat—and all out of sheer luck! The tenant, Mr. Goudsmit, has been collecting our mail. Out of good-will he wants us all to have our mail once we return from Switzerland! This has now been brought to my attention, after a long period of sitting in the dark. "The wretched Nazis are busy drinking tonight, no doubt," M.G. said to Mummy. They are purportedly celebrating the impressive success of submitting Jews to humiliations. What else have they to cheer for?

But I am secretly happy tonight too—for I have a treasure in my hands! I hugged and kissed M.G... Secretly, in the front office, M.G. handed over *the letter that has finally calmed my fears.*

"Margot. I cannot go to the Merwedeplein (our home address) again. It is too dangerous. But I saw an opportunity yesterday. I was walking past your home, and Mr. Goudsmit recognized me. He informed me that mail arrived for the Franks, would I be so kind to place it in the offices of the Franks, perhaps for after the war? I made sure he knew I did not know of your whereabouts. 'Hopefully they will return from Switzerland after the war...' I fabricated; He nodded and handed me this. I may go again once more, Margot. But only if it should happen again by chance. I do not want to seem overly eager for mail." She gave me the letter. This letter I am now holding in my hand, as I write with the other...

Here is the attached letter:
January 1943
Margot!

'Molahs!' My dearest friend in Holland! My long-awaited dream has been fulfilled! Australia is a beautiful country and the seaside cities just as I imagined, even more majestic and regal than my poor writing skills can describe. The mainland is filled with newcomers like me, eager for a vacation during these times. I have enlisted in the Preservation of the Species Corps, a new organization dedicated to assisting the threatened species off the shores of the Baltic and the Eastern European sea board. Australia is concerned the species of rare starfish will not survive harsh brutalities, such as over killing and gasoline spills. I have joined a team of explorers, and will soon arrive in the European mainland in hopes of aiding the starfish to regain strength and purpose so they don't become extinct. I am being trained by professional marine biologists, and I am part of a team of experts, though internationally not recognized as of yet. I hope I will be able to share my experiences of great success; our world needs to help endangered species and wildlife, even now, during a time of war.

I hope you are feeling well, Margot. I miss you. Here in Australia, few speak the wonderful language of our hometown, and my English (Aussie) is not so very honed, I'm afraid. I carry a dictionary when I travel inland. I have met other Europeans, so I am not alone here, in Australia.

My thoughts are with you. Take good care of yourself. Don't give in to harsh winters, when you know eventually spring will come. All my best wishes,

Mordechai

At first I thought the letter was so strange. What was Mordechai speaking of, with the mention of 'Australia,' 'The Preservation of the Species Corps,' training in marine biology? And then, I figured it out: the letter is written in code! Mordechai didn't want to alert the suspicions of the Germans, were they to read this letter, since it is addressed from Palestine, British territory! Mordechai did not want to give away sensitive information… This is how I translated the letter:

Molahs! = Shalom (it is spelled backwards)!
Australia= Palestine.
Mainland= Jerusalem and the other cities outside of the coastal area.
Vacation= escape from Nazi persecution.
Starfish= Jews.
Preservation of the Species Corps= a resistance group.
Threatened species= Jews.
Baltic/European seaboard= Poland, Czechoslovakia, Hungary etc.
Team of explorers= Resistance group, probably clandestine soldiers of some sort.
Professional marine biologists= Trained army personnel.

Mordechai is going to fight the Germans in some secret mission! He joined the resistance group in Palestine he often spoke about! He is an excellent candidate; he knows the areas well; he speaks the language; he can easily blend in. But he did not mention his trip, the hardships, his trials. What a man is this Mordechai! Who would have imagined such a plot? It seems suicidal to me. To take such grave risks; indeed, he is very brave. I have newfound respect for a man who carries his ideals into actions. I am so nervous for him! The enemy knows no mercy; nothing will stop them from annihilating him if he is discovered. What a mission—he is probably sleepless. He feels as though he can now do *something* to help his brothers in need, his mother in some God-forsaken country (if she is still alive), and his fellow Jews in suffering.

And to think he kept his word. "I won't be able to write for a long time." This does not mean that he won't write at all! I find his straightforwardness a nice respite from the monotony of uncertainty. Daily, we are faced with purported information, rumors, some grounded in fact, some not. He has given me new-found hope! Maybe he will be able to kill some German soldiers, aid the war effort. Maybe he will be able to free Jews in bondage, like Moses! Now I am becoming too much of a romantic, but I will allow myself this momentary luxury, even if I know I am possibly deluding myself…

How will he make it into the mainland? Parachute. Of course.

I have seen the Allies parachute into occupied Holland. Anne and I, in fact, saw them landing during an assault not too long ago. It is frightful to watch! How much more so to experience. Who knows where he will land? What if he falls behind enemy lines? The scenarios I can play out are numerous and each one sadly more tragic than the previous ones.

    A. He is caught by Russians. The Russians will not believe that he is *not* an enemy combatant. His German accent will betray him. This will lead to his execution. Perhaps if they shall feel an iota of mercy or doubt, they will send him to Siberia.

    B. Jews do not believe him. They do not aid him or listen to his directives (not so likely).

    C. He falls in the hands of the Nazis and is murdered, execution style.

D. He is captured by Nazi personnel, and they imprison him. Out of sheer brutality, they torture him until he expires.
E. His parachute fails, and he plunges to his death.
F. He drowns at sea.
G. He is captured and sent to a concentration camp as a Jew. He manages to conceal his clandestine mission from the Nazis, and they do not suspect he is a combatant.
H. He is captured, sent to a brutal labor camp. He is detained. Indefinitely. He becomes another statistic.
I. He succeeds and kills countless Germans and Nazis. He gathers Jews. He organizes a resistance. He heads the group of rogues and blows up Nazi headquarters. He sabotages trains, cargo, and frees Jewish prisoners. In a skirmish with the Nazis, he falls in battle. His legacy dies.
J. Mordechai succeeds and lands in German-occupied territory. He thinks he is in Russian-occupied territory. He realizes soon that he is outnumbered, and there is no one in sight who can support him. He flees to the forest where he tries to eke out an existence. He may fail. He may succeed. He is at the mercy of nature.

I could go on all night. But I believe I have left my nail beds in such shape as to warrant a reproof from Mrs. Van Pels.

One thing is for certain—I have a new reason to pray with greater concentration.

**

I feel Mordechai's arrival on the Continent is imminent. In my prayers I plead for his success, and I move on with my day. I'm in a much better mood these days.

Anne and I are becoming closer. She has changed a great deal since last year. She has begun praying with me. We take turns reading from the prayer book. Mummy and Daddy are pleased. They feel Anne will gain a great deal from conversing with God!

Anne is becoming more understanding with Mummy; they argue less now. I can't help but feel Anne and Mummy's miscommunications are the cause of bitterness between them. It seems their personalities are bouncing off each other's. But Anne is learning to put her selfishness aside. It is hard for her, she has confided this much...but she is slowly becoming a truly considerate daughter. She helps Mummy with the potato peeling, the housework, and the cooking. She does not involve herself so much with the adults anymore. She spends more time with Peter, in the attic. They work on cross-word puzzles together; they share their 'homework' assignments. Pim assigns homework in order to maintain our sanity!

Anne has finally menstruated too. This is a big deal for Mummy. She feels as though her baby is growing into a woman. Oddly enough, she has begun treating Anne like a young girl. When she fell ill with the flu, for nearly two weeks, Mummy was brought to life by her feelings of renewed motherhood. She boiled the milk. She prepared compresses, convinced Anne to swallow innumerable lozenges, and she even fluffed Anne's pillow—and with such grace and concern. It was as if she felt that *now* that Anne could not resist her, she could mother her the way she wanted to. Anne obliged. She was too weak to argue or resist. To Mummy's disappointment, Anne wanted *Pim* to kiss her good night, despite Mummy's obvious care and love throughout the day.

When Anne first saw blood in her undergarments, she had tears in her eyes. She proudly exhibited her prized evidence. I congratulated her. "You're a grown woman now, Anne!" I whispered to her. She beamed. This is all she wants to be—a beautiful young woman. She later confided in M.G. She could barely contain her excitement. This brought smiles to the female faces. She did not bring it up again, though. Perhaps she is a bit embarrassed from the men. They would never guess; men do keep to their own world, as do we women.

When I menstruated, I was barely twelve-years-old. Our biology instructor prepared us for this "monumental stage in female sexual development," to quote Mrs. Klein. I did not feel as though I was capable of having a child of my own, but the potential for such made me all the more curious about men and lovemaking. Whenever I read any account of lovemaking, I would store the information and create a mental picture of what it would be like. It all seemed so foggy because I did not have an object of desire upon whom to pin my lovely ideas about love. Oh. But that is changing.

Were it not for the war, Sytie might have been married. I am eighteen now too. Were I an Orthodox Jewish woman, I would have been under the wedding canopy (*chuppah*) by my eighteenth birthday. Last year, I would have stated, "Eighteen! That is too young." But I feel so old. I have as of now withdrawn such a thought. "Whenever love may knock on your door—answer it before you are left alone in your own home." This is not an original metaphor, but it will have to do…

And I am not surprised I used such a metaphor. Mordechai knocked on the door, a couple of days after we met. He gave me the tome of Jewish history I wrote about months ago. He wanted me to see his viewpoints, share his opinions. I thought he was being friendly, but I now see he wanted me to become a part of his world. He marked the entire book with comments. I felt as though I were sleeping with a part of him, each time I placed the book near my pillow, at bedside. His style was concise, sometimes witty, with a fine and elegant print. Some remarks were in Hebrew or Aramaic, from the Talmud perhaps, all of which I could not make any sense of. Other markings were annotations for his own study.

Even though I finished the book in less than a week, I kept it near my table, just to smell it. The whiff of his cologne excited my senses. A couple of times I awoke mid-night just to smell the pages. My nose was stuck in the book—but for 'unacademic' reasons! When I returned it, I unintentionally touched his index finger. I felt that touch down the entire length of my body. My heart raced! My cheeks are burning from this sweet memory. But I quickly attributed this to my quiet nature and my shyness. (This was certainly a part of the total experience of speaking to him, but unrelated to this very specific event!)

Being locked in this Back House has a way of becoming an alleyway into self-revelation and awareness. I would have loved to be near him then too. But my blind-sightedness…

I did not recognize my own desires. It was right there, yet I failed to see it, failed to reach for it. Now I hold on to the memories of what could have been and what yet might be.

***

Today's my birthday. Everyone's been a darling. Father wrote a sweet poem:

>Though you may ask what else am I to read,
>Know your Father is here for you, indeed.
>Through these hard times we will lean on each other,
>And wield strength and reliance; as a doting Father
>Everlasting and hopeful that you and I
>Will hold hands today, tomorrow; Nay— I shall not say good bye!
>For even when you are betrothed, married, or old and raggedy,
>I shall remain your loving and all-too doting 'Daddy'.

(Translated from the German.)

Mummy presented me with a new brassiere, the Van Pelses a beautiful fountain pen, Mr. Pfeffer a mirror with lovely brass engravings, and Peter handed me a wood carving of a jewelry box, "just the right size for your diary." M.G.'s gift was precious: new stockings. I desperately needed hosiery for the longest time. Most of my socks (and undergarments besides) are torn and in a state of disrepair. I am so excited to wear them; I don't want to ruin them. Anne's gift was very sweet: I did not do any housework today courtesy of Anne!

Before the war, Mummy and Daddy would spoil me to no end on my birthday. Each year I anticipated such grandness. But really, the lavish gifts, (and let's not forget the money!) clouded the love I should have felt from my parents. I looked forward to the gifts, not so much as to the expression of the person behind the new bicycle, or the new skirts, the laced-boots, or the fashionable brooch. What I am trying to say is very simple: I feel loved today more than I ever felt before the war, even though I received 'small' gifts in comparison. Father's poem really warmed me. Pim is such a darling. And a new brassiere! Before the war it was a necessity; today it is a treasure! And who would give young women hosiery for a birthday gift! A faux pas! (What nonsense is it all now…) Yet those considerations are so very subjective. Today, I am more than proud to say: hosiery is a very thoughtful gift!

And I am beginning to appreciate the concept of hiring housekeepers. Imagine—living an entire life without ever cleaning after anyone, even yourself! Perhaps that is the mark of a very spoiled person… or a very fortunate one!

Or a very busy person. But I shall be neither. I am not afraid of getting my hands a little dirty. So long as I have enough soap to rinse them later…

This of course, brings me to think about those dirty diapers I rinsed in the maternity ward. At first I thought I shouldn't be able to bear the indignity. But, as soon as I rinsed them, once, twice and again for a third time, the routine rubbed away the initial disgust. And so it was here, cleaning all the greasy dishes; the basin in the W.C. was constantly cruddy. I knew everyone's 'leftovers' by heart! I became catty and short-tempered each time I heard the endless complaints of those who imposed themselves on me… In short, I was terribly crabby at becoming a housewife to an adopted family without my consent.

I have changed since then. I don't think too much before I get to work. I help Mummy, especially with the chores that are harder for her, such as rinsing the pots and scrubbing the floors. I do not utter too many complaints and wait for some quiet time to regain composure. Since the daytime must be as peaceful as possible, I try to remain in good spirits; the evening is hard enough with all the chatter at dinner time.

I find the less I judge the others the easier I sleep at night. The more I let go of my own ideas of who said what, and who was right and who was wrong and why they were wrong and why they may possibly be right, the more space I have in my own mind for my own thoughts and whether these thoughts are right or wrong, good or bad, helpful or harmful. Once I would immerse myself in a book; now I pump out the bickering and retain my own peace of mind. This is a practice most difficult to achieve!

I have moments that I am completely overwhelmed by such utter noise that I feel a migraine come on. I find a way to keep busy. If it is night, I leave to the Warehouse and file papers. If I can't do that, then I will write letters in Latin to my ghost-professor. (I am in correspondence with a professor of Latin. The professor thinks I am B., who mails my work.) I will try to speak in Latin and write directly what I think, instead of mapping out my letter in German and then translating. This arduous task keeps my mind churning; so much so, that my incoming migraine leaves me, and I am too tired to hear any noise or make sense of anything I see. I refer to this as 'working my head out of a headache.'

***

Perceptions—are they real?

I am spending too much time reading. I am not relating enough, not to people or to my locket-diary. I am so alone in my thoughts, and I begin to doubt my perceptions of people, specifically of Mordechai. I think I'm reading too much into my relationship with Mordechai. After all, we did not share so much contact with each other. He was more of a mentor. He never declared his love for me. He did not kiss me or touch me or compliment me… How I wish now that he had! Then I wouldn't be alone. I would know perhaps that love waits for me as it waits for so many girls my age. And I would not have cause to doubt. Only wonder. But now I remain alone.

And all this I doubt because love has come at last to our hideaway Back House.

Love—at last.

Anne has become attached to Peter in ways we didn't anticipate. She visits him very often. (Even some of the adults are commenting on her behavior. She ignores them, thankfully.) They are becoming close friends. It seems they have begun to take notice of one another out of pity or even out of loneliness. A bond is beginning to form. At first, I was taken by surprise because initially neither Peter nor Anne took much notice of each other. Anne thought he was silly and odd. Peter thought she was too gregarious and brazen. They were classically prejudiced. But so much has changed since last year. Peter's self-esteem has improved—thanks to Pim. And Anne has matured, quite a bit, and hence her attitudes and behavior are less threatening to Peter. It seems they have been walking toward this path, but we never saw it coming. Truth be told, he did not flirt with Anne, as most boys did before the war. This, come to think of it, is the oddest thing of all! How two people, who otherwise would never have much to do with one another, have now become close friends! Anne's mood is so very much improved. I am glad for that—since her cheery disposition has a way of rubbing off…

Oh. But this new circumstance in our secret hideaway is creating some 'news' (for the adults) and a jolt for me. It is fair to say that I am partly envious that she has the ability to share her thoughts with someone she can speak with, here in the present form. (I can't even write to Mordechai, let alone share my dreams with him!) But if I would be able to finally share that intimacy with a man, I would want that 'speech' to be a silent one. The gaze. The understanding. I am so very quiet—I think of love as a respect for one's inner peace.

Anne approached me and blatantly asked me, "Are you jealous of me, Margot?" She is concerned that I may have a hard time, being the elder, and yet all alone, while she, the younger, is so close with Peter. I had to think for a while. Truth be told, I feel more self-pity than anything else. I am not jealous of their relationship because the type of relationship they share is not the one I seek. Anne and Peter's relationship suits them very well, but were I to converse with Peter I would not feel emotionally (or intellectually) satiated. I would not gain as much as I would have loved. And besides, I do not feel the strong attraction I so desire (and am slowly beginning to recognize that I had to Mordechai). Anne always had the boys surround her, ever since I can remember. I remember Peter Schiff so well; the days she spent with him—and she was much younger than I at the time! They were inseparable; child-lovers if one may call it that. And then *too* I was alone. I have often felt estranged from Anne— not only our age difference, but our temperament and our circle of friends have always been different. It is here in the hideaway by the canal that we three, Peter, Anne, I, have somewhat become one unit—"the children." Now it is more like "Anne and Peter" (friends) and Margot (alone). This feeling that I may never know a lover fills me with *self-pity*.

Why must I now suffer burning heartaches for a man (and my only imaginings lead me to the one man I have ever known with the potential for that love) in addition to the difficult life of a hideaway Jew? This bitterness is palpable—so much so that Anne took notice immediately and took my case to her heart. Oh sweet Anne!

I do not want Anne to miss any opportunities. She deserves love, even if I am never to know much in the way of lovers. She deserves a chance, *without* the burden of guilt. With such in mind I wrote her a letter; I couldn't trust myself to speak about such painful thoughts (without the threat of my self-pity erupting into shameful tears).

This is what I wrote. (I did not reveal anything about Mordechai. Not even Mummy knows about him.)

Anne, when I said yesterday that I was not jealous of you I was only fifty percent honest. It is like this; I'm jealous of neither you nor Peter. I only feel a bit sorry that I haven't found anyone yet (a partial lie, but understandable), *and am not likely for the time being, with whom I can discuss my thoughts and feelings. But I should not grudge it to you for that reason. One misses enough here anyway, things that other people just take for granted.*

On the other hand, I know for certain that I would never have got so far with Peter, anyway, because I have the feeling that if I wished to discuss a lot with anyone, I should want to be on rather intimate terms with him. I would want to have the feeling that he understood me through and through, without having to say much. But for that reason it would have to be someone whom I felt was my superior intellectually, and that is not the case with Peter. But I can imagine it being so with you and Peter.

You are not doing me out of anything which is my due; do not reproach yourself in the least on my account. You and Peter can only gain by the friendship.

I don't want to doubt myself, my feelings, or my hopes. It is true that now I am unable to discuss much with Mordechai. Perhaps he has some strong feelings for me, but did he not follow through with his emotions because he knew he would escape? Perhaps he did not want to cause unnecessary harm?

It is draining to play emotional guessing games. For now, Mordechai is a good friend. I shall do better remaining most objective about him! Is it possible?

I now tell myself, "Good luck, Margot!"

A short prayer: Please God in Heaven who sees the world as an Eagle can see her prey—

Do not let me die without knowing the depth of love; without the sound of a lover's voice; without the knowledge of a soul-mate; without my half-soul's declaration of heart.

***

Are we Jews really a race?

I have been reading a great deal on religion. Christianity and Islam both draw their constructs of belief from Judaism. There is no Christian or Muslim who denies that the Hebrews were chosen by the Lord as a nation of holy priests and holy men. This strengthens my commitment to my own religion—if Christians and Muslims recognize my heritage, then

I embrace it. With both arms. Despite my lack of complete knowledge and my many, many questions.

How I do wish I knew more about my religion—and not from books! Celebrating the Sabbath is one of the Ten Commandments, yet we do not keep the Sabbath as per Jewish Law. The Festival of the Tabernacle, where a Jew eats, sleeps, and learns in a *succah* (a tent of sorts) is truly a remarkable holiday. Men pray in the synagogue, return and celebrate with a hearty meal in a makeshift 'house'—and all this to commemorate the exodus from Egypt. And of course, Passover. The festival of Matzos. Jews teach their children the cruel history of slavery and bondage and the redemption of the Hebrews in an awesome night, called the Seder Eve. A child eats bitter herbs to recollect the 'bitterness' of the bondage. Pregnant mothers together with all the women (who must also partake) sing the songs of the Hallelujah!

Passover by the Goslars... the memory ignites such nostalgia! Baby Gaby would chew the matzos and say, "Mummy, I want more!" Daddy would pour me the four glasses of wine, and Hanneli would ask the "four questions." The matzo soup that evening had a special flavor. The horseradish—I never ate too much!

With the emancipation of Europe's Jews, nearly one hundred years ago or so, many Jews abandoned their religion and embraced the nationalism of their sponsor countries. We are Dutch Jews, not Jewish Dutch. When we lived in Germany, before the Nuremberg Laws and before Hitler's ascension, we were Germans of the Jewish faith. But it seems God has other plans for us! Today, we are Jews and nothing else. I am determined to learn as much as I possibly can about what it means to be a Jew since this is my fate and my destiny. Hitler made all of Europe the most race-conscious of all people; I am no exception.

I do struggle with the concept of Jews as a "race." I think this is inaccurate. Jews can trace their origin to the twelve tribes of Israel; whereas other groups of people, who are often categorized as a race, may not be able to trace their beginnings to one particular family. In that sense, the Jews are more of an extended family, a close-knit clan that has grown exponentially.

Anne has been drawing family trees of the royal families of Europe. I wish I were able to trace my family tree to one of the Twelve Tribes!

It does amaze me, when I read the Bible, how incredibly faithful Abraham, Isaac, and Jacob were. They were able to 'speak' with God, so-to-speak. How I would love to converse with my Creator! I would love to ask Him questions. I have so many:

Why are we to suffer like this? Why are Jews persecuted and made to feel ashamed of being called 'Jews?'

Why do we have to fear the Germans, the probable descendants of Esau, today, years after the Bible was written?

Why do we not have a Moses to lead us out of our misery, as the Jews of Egypt had? Why is today's Pharaoh's army succeeding at choking the Jews in chambers of steel, dying with tongues flailing and stomachs churning?

Why do we not have a Savior?

But even as I ask these questions, I am ashamed for having doubt in God's justice. Job, who suffered much more than I can ever imagine, did not question God, nor did he waver in his trust and loyalty.

I have no right, but I am so very curious to know what churns in the cosmos.

The universe is an incredible mystery. The laws governing this world fascinate and intrigue me to no end. Yet the more I read and the more I learn about the universe and this tiny planet known as Earth, the more confused I inevitably become.

How can it be that an individual can overcome the powers set forth by gravity and by the movements of the planets? (How is it that the sun and moon "stood still," simply because Joshua exhorted them to do so?)

And yet, despite this ability, how is it that he remains so petty and inconsequential?

How can it be that the greatest of all creations, the Human Species, is the feeblest animal roaming this planet?

Why do people refuse to admit their small stature before all this greatness?

What is the purpose of the Jew in the ever-unfolding patterns of life on Earth?

How is my life, so insignificant (and paltry) in comparison to the cosmos, yet so incredibly real and larger than life to me, in my mind, in my body, and in my essence? What is my purpose as a Jewish girl? How can I fulfill my mission when I am forbidden to walk the streets, let alone create a life for myself?

What are the rules governing life—who lives and who dies, who can see and who cannot, who shall remain unknown and who shall be known for all eternity?

These and many more are the questions I have.

For now I am searching for answers in my studies. I read nearly everything: Physics, Algebra, Geometry, Trigonometry, Geography, Biology, and Economics, Literature (Dutch, German, French, and English), the Bible and medical texts as well. For the most part, I find that the vast knowledge of both the sciences and the arts lead one to conclude that God must have placed this knowledge as a means to search and find His Essence in this World.

Yet His Essence is ever so elusive!

We can never truly *know* God's ways. If we did, we would be God! Mordechai pointed this out. At the time, I thought he was repeating something he was taught. Now I am beginning to see the wisdom behind this profound thought.

I am full of absolute wonder when I study physics and medicine. If one studies the human eye alone, one inescapably and intuitively grasps that only the Mastermind of all Humanity could have created such perfection. I felt especially close to God when I volunteered in the hospital. From the woman's egg and the man's seed came forth an entire individual. This is a miracle! And for that reason I treasured the maternity ward—the feeling that the Lord was with me was ever-present. All that I have ever read, especially this past year, has not delighted or remotely satiated me as my little 'turtle-baby'; the beautiful boy born on that wonderful day...

As a woman I feel especially close to God, knowing I have within me the secret power to nourish a life, and that God entrusted me, a woman, with that ability is so every humbling and wonderfully fulfilling.

It is true I can be a professor or any other brainy person. But learning and reading is only a means for me. The end I so desire is feeling that closeness to my Source.

I do not have the answers to my questions, and my faith wavers. I won't lie.

But each time I glance at the azure sky I am reassured that there is rhyme and reason.

When the sun blinds me and peeks through the hopeless sky I am reminded of baby Gaby's smile.

I recall the babies and the nursery. The labor and delivery department. The hospital. Rebeka. Mrs. Strauss. Dr. Mann. Sophiia.

And I hold on to my dream of nursing laboring women and newborn babies.

A spiritual rebirth reignites my faith.

I hold on to these—because they remind me of the beauty of God's world.

How I would love to begin living my dream! I desperately want to begin my life outside the confines of these walls, this desperate house. I feel I am behind, in my life's goal, in this 'back house.' How I wish I could move forward!

***

A poem during moments of reverie:

For God Laments…
Your Cry
Engulfs the Sea
The clouds carry your Tears
From this finite Ocean
Into Infinity.

***

I feel I owe the Van Pels an apology. Firstly, I have not depicted Mrs. Van Pels in a fair light. It is true she cares a great deal for her delicate finery, but she cannot be blamed for missing her luxuries. After all, Auguste was habituated to the finer things in life, as I have been. Perhaps I may not have been as outspoken as she. Perhaps I have my vanities too, which is why I pointed them out in Mrs. Van Pels. Truly, is it not vain to assume that school work should continue here in this secret hideaway? (Anne told me she named our hideout "The Secret Annexe", which is quite apt.) Is this not an assumption? It is a positive one and one I adopt every day and one I would never reconsider, but, in all honesty it *is* a form of expectation, is it not? Solomon himself said, "Vanities of vanities, all is vanity." One can then say that even studying math and science can be an exercise in vanity—and by this I mean uselessness or worthlessness. Unless, unless.

Unless one utilizes these studies to gain some type of wisdom about larger aspects of the world, and by this I mean creation, the purpose of life, the wonders of God.

On an entirely different note, Peter invited me to join him and Anne for conversation. I went a couple of times, out of boredom, loneliness, and a tad of curiosity, only to discover that I may be intruding on the two love-buds. It is better to remain here, in the front office, alone and with my thoughts, than with Peter and Anne, trying to escape from the adults and their comments.

Truly it is degrading to be treated like a child when I feel like anything but a 'child.' I have long since outgrown my dependence and my feelings of insecurity. But we all must play our roles, out of respect if anything, and this should be enough.

I can see why Anne takes to Peter. But I do not think they would have been close to one another were it not for our sensitive situation. Father mentors Peter all the time, and he thinks he is a fine lad. Father's approval matters a great deal to Anne, and he is a very good judge of character.

Of all of us here, in the "Secret Annexe," it is Father who remains the most steadfast. Even when others have succumbed to bursts of anger or deep anxiety, Father has remained bold, calm, and logical. He possesses such a kind and thoughtful spirit. He is, of all the men I have met, by far superior in character. I am proud to have him as my Pim; I am proud to call him "Father."

Mother and I have always been close. This has been both a blessing and, at times, not such a blessing. When Mummy shares with me her very personal woes, they become my own. And in this way I have grown beyond my years. However, when Mummy and I share good times and wonderfully revealing tête-à-tête, then we are good friends and we feel truly connected. In this way I am still bonded to her, as I was in the womb. The umbilical cord is attached. And therein I feel loved.

Oddly enough, I am still my own person. I do not share the same opinions nor do I share Mummy's every interest. (She likes to knit dresses and cook, but I prefer to play tennis, swim outdoors, and practice advanced geometry.) But we are not meant to be mirror images of each other.

Mummy has been in a state of despair for a very long time now. Her fears of discovery are preventing her from experiencing relief or quietude. Instead, she is a bundle of nerves. And Mrs. Van Pels seems to aggravate her sensitive nerves with great success.

Father has never uttered any regret (with regards to inviting the Van Pels to join us). Quite the opposite: he feels responsible for his fellow Jew in suffering, and he understands that sharing close quarters with others will inevitably result in some type of squabbling. He is our schoolmaster and Peter's foster parent. This has endeared Father even more to us all.

Mummy suffers pangs of guilt for "leaving the Goslars behind." Father constantly tries to explain to Mummy that Mrs. Goslar's "situation" (her pregnancy) prevented her from remaining confined...and Baby Gaby... she was a toddler at the time...

Anne and I are growing closer, but there is still a distance between us. I don't think she trusts me enough; she assumes I will mock her or won't understand her deepest feelings. But this is a misunderstanding on her part, since I am ready to hear all she has to say; I am open, although I am closed the entire day, keeping to myself, quiet and altogether mouse-like.

I have become this way, in part, to protect myself from criticism. I saw the way the adults encroached on Anne's private actions or every word she dared mutter. If she joked around a little too much for someone's sensitivities, then a proceeding and hearing followed. The onslaughts kept coming. Each time I witnessed Mrs. Van Pels or Mr. Van Pels (and the dentist) grow impatient, I grew more and more introverted, fearful of criticism and of being judged. I wanted to throw fits too; I had moments I wanted to mutter to myself or ignore my chores. But I had to rewire my core reaction to suit the sensitivity of the adults. I did not always succeed. If I reacted negatively, it was mostly towards Anne (whom I secretly blamed for my withdrawn and angry attitude).

This slowly changed as we grew out of our own shells. I buried myself with studies and started to follow Father's example and make use of myself. Writing helps. Sharing my thoughts with Anne helps too. Anne's attitude has changed dramatically in the last year; one can hardly recognize her from pre-war Anne. We have learned to detach ourselves from our parents and their reactions (mostly Mummy) in order to protect ourselves from all the negativity of the adult scene. So, if Mummy and Mrs. Van Pels begin one of their many political rows, Anne and I will not react with the same anxiety or frustration as we did in the beginning. I quietly leave the room, and now Anne and Peter spend more time in the attic (in the evening) than with the family in the dining room (so they avoid the quarrels as well). It is a sad, but universal truth that spending too much time with another person will lead to quarreling and bickering. And that is mainly because people need breadth of space to grow. Yet, in spite of it all, Anne has grown into a young woman, and I have done so as well. In spite of it all, we have learned a great deal about ourselves, how we want to conduct our lives and our homes after the war…

Anne would like to pursue a career in writing or journalism. She is serious about becoming a published author. She believes writing is a way to make a mark in this world. I just want to live in Palestine, in a country all my own. Once I am safe from Hitler and this war is all over, I want to continue learning medicine, especially gynecology and obstetrics. Becoming a midwife, a purveyor of life, will help me dispel my fears of death. And in this way, I will live my life pursuing life. And perhaps the thought of death will escape me, even if it is for a single sweet moment.

***

I don't know if I can do this anymore. Again. Other break-in. Petty burglars. But this time it was far more serious. Everyone's bowels loosened to the extent that the makeshift potties stunk so badly, and we had to remain in our positions until we had the all-clear. The police rattled the cupboard door (the entry way) so many times, we felt that with each bang and each tug the noose around our necks was tightening. The flatulence in the room was unbearable. The sense of smell became a curse. I lost my appetite for well over a day. Who can tolerate the stench of fear?

We have lived in this hideaway for so long now that we have become lax in our vigilance. There is no way to determine if anyone has discovered our secret.

God may have protected us for this long, but will we remain lucky?

I don't want to go into the particulars of that terrible day, but I learned all too well the immediacy of discovery.

Another fear: Anne's diary. Since the Queen urged the Dutch to keep close records of their war-time experiences (for publication after all this is done with), Anne has been extra-careful to detail all the experiences of her "Secret Annexe." I've helped her with a bit of the editing and re-writing. But now, we are afraid of its discovery or that it may fall into the wrong hands. Anne is adamant that her diary remain a hidden treasure of this war, and "If my diary goes, I go with it!"

A declaration. It all seems to be most fitting—that the adults should right away think of Anne's diary. She has made it known to all. But I have been so secretive about mine! No one remembers that I have one too. I have been documenting our experiences since our first day here. But I have a way of becoming invisible, and it seems my effort at privacy has prevailed. I took few measures at concealing certain people's identity. Namely, our saviors. Anne's declaration of 'till death do us part' helped me reconsider my commitment to secrecy. Like Anne, then, I will take my diary whither I go.

***

So much for trying to remain in my own world. Mrs. Van Pels and I had our first very serious confrontation. And to think it was all concerning red-nail color....

The story goes like this:

Late last night I placed my Bible on the dining room table and forgot about it. In the morning I searched the entire house for it. And it was gone.

I asked each individual separately.

"Have you seen my Bible?"

Mrs. Van Pels-no.

The dentist-hm?

Father-try the library.

Peter-I think I saw it near the kitchen table.

Anne-sorry.

Mummy-that's odd, I could have sworn I had just seen it here.

Well, it just so happened I went to scrub the kitchen floor, and there was Mouschi, chewing on ...my Bible! And what should grace the front cover but stains of red nail lacquer. It seems someone used the BIBLE as a 'mat' to protect the table cloth. I was irate!

"Mrs. Van Pels. This is a desecration! The Bible should not be used for anything!"

"Mrs. Frank, is this how you taught your daughters to speak to elders?"

My Mummy was drawn into the altercation.

"My Margot never says anything forcefully unless she is in the right, Mrs. Van Pels."

"Humfh. Well, you are right… I am sorry. It was late last night and I did not realize it was a Bible. I never intended…"

I felt a bit sorry that I had judged her unfavorably; (I did not dispense 'benefit of the doubt'), but in all honesty: doesn't someone realize what is in front of his very eyes?

I withdrew to my room and tried to scrape off the red color. The leather front-cover is now scratched, etched with a fork and knife.

The page Mouschi was chewing was an interesting portion from the Pentateuch. I re-read the section as I tried to undo the teeth marks…

Deuteronomy, chapter 30. Verses 11-20.

On the side-lines, the commentators wrote, "The Offer of Life or Death."

I wrote the words here:

11 Now what I am commanding you today is not too difficult for you or beyond your reach. 12 It is not up in heaven, so that you have to ask, "Who will ascend into heaven to get it and proclaim it to us so we may obey it?" 13 Nor is it beyond the sea, so that you have to ask, "Who will cross the sea to get it and proclaim it to us so we may obey it?" 14 No, the word is very near you; it is in your mouth and in your heart so you may obey it.

15 See, I set before you today life and prosperity, death and destruction. 16 For I command you today to love the LORD your God, to walk in his ways, and to keep His commands, decrees and laws; then you will live and increase, and the LORD your God will bless you in the land you are entering to possess.

17 But if your heart turns away and you are not obedient, and if you are drawn away to bow down to other gods and worship them, 18 I declare

to you this day that you will certainly be destroyed. You will not live long in the land you are crossing the Jordan to enter and possess.

19 This day I call heaven and earth as witnesses against you that I have set before you life and death, blessings and curses. Now choose life, so that you and your children may live 20 and that you may love the LORD your God, listen to His voice, and hold fast to Him. For the LORD is your life, and He will give you many years in the land He swore to give to your fathers, Abraham, Isaac and Jacob.

The Lord tells His nation that the Land of Israel (Palestine today) will belong to them so long as they do not "bow down to other gods and worship them." Today, we are suffering because our ancestors did not obey the Lord. He set before us all life and prosperity. Death and destruction. The latter is the inevitability of idol-worship (and other evils) and the former the reward for abiding by God's decrees. God Himself tells the nation of Israel that "the LORD is your life." Yet the ancestors of all the Jews today chose death. Ousted by the Lord into exile, they began the long journey into deep despondency. In their despair they began to desire the words of the Lord. In exile, the Jew will become so very thirsty for the words of God. They will regain their desire to listen to His decrees, because they will realize, after all, that it is God who is the Giver, the ultimate Father who seeks only the benefit of His children.

Can it be that today we suffer because we do not have Palestine, or rather *"Eretz Yisrael?"* If only we listened to God and chose life! He tells us the better choice, "Now choose life!" Were we foolish? Did we, like churlish children, think it best to follow our own path?

The Lord does not want to inflict harm on His children, just as a parent does not want to spank his child if he has spoken out of line. But sometimes, for the benefit of the child, the father reprimands him or even lets him realize how disobedience leads him toward self-destruction.

Is that an apt metaphor? How much is the act of God? How much is the act of man?

How much can be blamed upon God—at what point does humanity's responsibilities begin?

Sometimes parents must intervene in their children's lives for their own benefit. I wonder if God will intervene in mine. And I hope we share the same vision, and if not today, then perhaps tomorrow? If not now, then perhaps in a time soon to follow?

We, Jews of Amsterdam, of Poland, of all of Europe, are living the Biblical prophesies, are we not? Afraid of the sound of our own breath, we are driven out of our towns… into pitiless crucibles of faith… the heavens bear witness to our martyred brethren, and the earth swallows the blood of innocents…just as they witnessed the call of God then… they witness our call for mercy today.

If we only had Palestine! Germany ousted the Jews. With each successive territory Germany inherited a greater "Jewish Problem." What to do with all those Jews? "Ship them out to sea!" But the world's countries had no interest in opening their doors. "Ship them back to sea!" Where are all those Jews today? I tremble to think… I tremble to write the words *concentration camps. Death camps. Labor camps. The East.*

How taxing it all seems! But if the punishments are so severe, then the *rewards* must be immense! There must be a balance, for God is the Lord of the Just…

And who is to say that God sanctions the severity of our punishment? Do not Satan's energies flow through mankind, out of their own volition, out of their own free will? God did not force Adam to sin, nor did He refrain from giving him the chance to fail. Mankind will decide for itself if their mentor will be Satan or if it will be the Lord Himself and His Servants (Abraham and Moses). Who knows where Satan's cult will lead us. We have yet to discover the capacity for such evil. Perhaps we are all living through this experiment of human nature and of human accountability. I hope and pray we choose the better path… Certainly one can assume goodness will follow from the source of good, and one dares not contemplate the possibilities of its opposite trajectory. I tremble to think that perhaps the wheels have been set into motion.

I tremble to think that perhaps we are in the midst of a catastrophic paradigm shift— from our innocent belief in the central goodness of our own character to the terrifying prospect that we cannot sustain a just society based on the strengths of humanity alone. There must be a higher call for justice, one based on Divine moral grounds, not *human* moral grounds.

"So long as we see our human strengths as our only source of guiding embers, then we will stand in a half-lit world." Mordechai's words. At the time, I didn't understand the deeper implications. Now I do.

Germany. The most advanced society. *Ethical* people! We placed our trust in people—and people now threaten our lives! How ironic and maddening a thought!

We must take note of our weaknesses: our inability to make sound judgments, our weaknesses of character and of thought, our poor ability to overcome lust and deep-rooted aggression, our all-too delicate temper, insecurity and petty self-interests and our inability to contain our anger and our animosity. In the wake of this terrible war I tremble to think that our very lives are in the hands of people such as the Germans, who have embraced a cult of sanctioned bloodletting, in the name of utter intolerance for anything related to or reminiscent of the Jew.

Hitler was not the first to seek our annihilation. (In the Book of Esther, Haman the Aggagite shared his vision. Hitler was not as forth coming as Haman, though.) We thought Hitler sought to humiliate the Jews. We thought his sole desire was total separation of Jew and Gentile. Of de-influence. Hence the removal of Jews from Germany proper and from high offices (in all realms of society) of influence. Hence the Nuremberg Laws.

Oh. We knew he was a thief of monumental proportions. The "Aryanization" (*Arisierung*) of property was nothing but legalized theft. (The transfer of businesses from Jew to Gentile for less than a fraction of its worth.)

We thought he wished to separate the "pure" races (notably the Aryan race) from the inferior races (Gypsies and of course, the 'dirty Jew'). Jews are well-accustomed to living in ghettos amidst hardships. We could have lived with this until war's end. But now, rumors of *gassing en masse* have surfaced, and our futile belief in the morality and ethics of the German Race has evaporated, so much so that the noise in our heads threatens to topple us in complete capitulation. We have been deceived by our beliefs in humanity. We have been too enamored with Goethe and with Mahler, with Humanism and with Nietzsche's tenets. To Nietzsche's people, God is no longer alive. German philosophy paved the way for such godlessness. And we are now witness to the after-effects, to the consequences of such death

117

purveying philosophies. The human mind is not to be trusted. Philosophy is all-too-capable of becoming the pitfall of the feeble-minded.

And we Jews are the mice in this terrible experiment.

The propaganda machine's wheels have been set in place, and now we see it spinning.

Perhaps the Jew will teach the world the destructive power of hatred… the Jew will be the vehicle through which the world will learn tolerance—or destruction. And there is nothing glorious in dying.

How I tremble to think of all the suffering of my people! The Lord felt our pain in Egypt, and surely I will follow in the path of the Lord. I, too, feel their pain, and I am sickly fearful that I may partake in this painful experiment.

Is this not a good time for redemption?

How can I bring about my *own* personal redemption? How I do wish to unshackle myself from the burdens of my people, from our colossal suffering at the hands of a brutal and godless people…

Is the *Torah* so far out of my reach? Will the Bible help me find peace?

Is everything Mordechai taught me true?

How I want to believe that it is not so far out of our reach! The Lord says so Himself, does he not? It is not in the stars or far out across the seas, but in our very hearts… We know what is expected of us, for it is in our minds. We know what the Lord has intended, for it is etched in our souls.

In my soul I will find the answers to my questions. I will also find the strength. And if I will not, somehow He will help me. I know He will. He promised this too…

Perhaps God Himself will open our ears; for years of exile have obstructed the sounds of our beating hearts, crying, "Hear O Israel! The Lord Our God…The Lord, is One!"

***

What a mess! Anne confided in me, and I offered some advice I believed would benefit her. But instead, my ideas all but backfired.

Anne and Peter for some time now have been increasingly affectionate. It appears they are "necking" (Father's term) in the attic. Father does not want Anne to be in any compromised situations. He warned her to be careful around Peter, to show restraint, to be, in short, unresponsive to certain gestures. He doesn't want Anne to encourage Peter. (I overheard most of the conversation. Yes. My nosy habits have not entirely disappeared… especially here; my habit has now become my nature, by default. Rather unfortunate I say.) Above all, Father doesn't want Anne to take her relationship with Peter "too seriously." Anne was upset for a while; she felt Father was burdening her with his authority, an authority she feels she is now ready to do without.

"I'm only fourteen Margot, but I am much more mature than most girls my age! You know that! I want Father and Mother to trust me when I go upstairs. I don't want them to tell me what to do, especially not with Peter!"

"But they *are* your parents, Anne; what are you going to do?"

"I don't feel they should pry in this way. I want them to trust me. I want Father to feel he can have faith in his daughter. I want them to treat me like an independent individual."

We sat on my bed for a while and discussed her feelings toward Peter and her feelings toward respecting Daddy and Mummy. She said she feels for Peter and loves to be around him and that most probably their connection at this point is not one she can let go of so easily. "But I'm not in love."

"Daddy is not asking you to say goodbye to Peter. He simply is asking you to maintain certain boundaries when you are with him. One thing usually leads to another, and our situation here, which is indefinite, can lead to that point very quickly Anne. Daddy is just trying to protect you. You are his *daughter*. It is entirely understandable."

Anne took my words to heart.

"I don't want to be at that point either, Margot. You know I would never—"

"Anne. That's what we all say in the beginning. But desperation and longing dictate differently…"

"I'm different. I know I am. I have a strong character, and Peter would never do something indecent. You know he wouldn't Margot!"

"People get caught up in their emotions. There's no real way to know what will happen until it's too late."

"Tell, me Margot. What do you think I should do?"

I had to think for a moment. Anne was so confused. I wanted to help her.

"Anne. I don't really know, because I have never been in your shoes. But this is what I think you *should* do. Write a letter to Daddy. Make it clear that you are not a regular fourteen-year-old girl. Tell him how much you want him to trust you, and tell him that you will always seek his counsel. Tell him how you feel. Explain to Daddy just how much you need Peter and how much he means to you. Maybe he'll understand you better. Maybe."

Anne thanked me and ran to her room. I was hopeful the results would be …. positive.

I have no idea what Anne wrote in that letter, but the expression on Daddy's face! One cannot describe how pained he was, disappointed, crestfallen. They sat in the room crying. Both of them. Together. Over a letter! I have no idea what she wrote because she swore to 'start a new leaf' and she tore the letter. I am worried I may have been a part of this fiasco, but I am afraid to ask.

Anne didn't reveal the *content* of the letter, but she did say, "I was unfair to Pim. I may have been too indelicate in some regards. I should have given it to you to read, Margot. You probably would have changed a couple of the phrases, edited my words, something. No matter. Let's forget this!"

I took notice, however, that Anne did not shoot up the stairs like her usual self since that day.

***

Het Achterhuis. The Back House. That is the title of Anne's prospective book. She will base the book on her diary. She is thrilled!

Will I be able to do the same?

No. I can't share everything I feel with strangers.

Maybe when I'm old, I'll show it to my granddaughter. When I no longer feel such subjectivity, when I am too close to dying to really care so much what other people think.

On another note: I finally told Anne I want to be a midwife in Palestine.

"Why would you want to do that?"

I couldn't explain the depth of my thoughts. I only said,

"Anne. This is what I believe I am destined to be and where I am destined to live."

"You don't want to live in Amsterdam after the war?! My God, Margot! Don't you love this country?"

"Maybe I do, but that doesn't matter. We belong in Palestine. It is our country. It will be our country."

"But Arabs live there, and the British have the mandate."

"I know. But we will be able to change that. If we all move there together and let the world know that the country belongs to us."

Anne retorted, indignantly, "But you already have a country: Holland."

"Anne. If we were Dutch and not merely Jews, we wouldn't be in hiding, would we? So how much is this country *ours*? And don't forget, Anne, Jews have always lived there too."

"But what if there are wars in Palestine? What would you do?"

"Then at least we would have a Jewish army to *fight* for our right to live, instead of living and *avoiding* any confrontation with our enemies!"

"There is no way to know what will happen to you here or there!" She slapped her knee in frustration.

"Then at least I will be buried in my ancestor's land and not in some strange land…"

"How could you be so morose, Margot! You shouldn't speak that way. It is too serious!"

She broke off the conversation…

Later on, Anne returned with a sad expression in her eyes. She held my shoulder and said:

"Whatever you do Margot. I know you will succeed. And as long as you are happy. And fulfilled. I wish you luck!"

We then spoke about the latest film to come out in theatre, our plans for after the war.

How I want her to fully understand why I am gravitating toward Palestine! Why I feel my calling is midwifery!

But I did not want to seem too dull.

And so I did not let her know.

***

Stifling heat! I can barely concentrate…and to think that only last week the W.C. was clogged! Imagine the smell of sweat, sauna-like heat, and the stench of sewage permeating the hideaway! We were spared that much. Outside: paradise. Long to be there.

***

There is hope for freedom—at last. D-day!

Anne squeezed my hand. "I can't believe the invasion is real!" Raptly, we listened to General Eisenhower on the radio. If he were in front of me right now, I would kiss him like the papa in the delivery room—on both cheeks, holding his face in my hands. "Thank you," I would say in English. And then I would hug all the strappy soldiers. "Thank you, too!"

They landed in Normandy. There were many casualties, but so far, the Americans are showing the Germans they have with whom to contend!

For so long now country after country capitulated to the Nazi juggernaut. Not anymore.

Things are about to change.

We are in a new phase of this war, and I feel the tables are turning for the hateful Germans who have spewed nothing but hatred and gore on this continent, on this country, on this city and on its inhabitants.

Welcome Americans! We pray God will be with you!

I wonder if Mordechai is safe; perhaps he will join the American soldiers?

This is all too wonderful; I will have a hard time sleeping tonight from all this excitement!

There is renewed reason to hope that I may return to school in September! (or October).

I detect a smile on my face.

And I pray for the success of the Americans!

Ps. Mrs. Van Pels kissed her husband passionately in front of us all tonight. She could not contain her elation. Peter turned colors. Poor boy! And the dentist looked on, vicariously enjoying the moment. Father folded his hands, and Mummy didn't seem to care; she is too happy! Anne and I smiled at one another. We held hands for a while longer.

***

Birthdays passed, Whitsun passed too. (The Pentecost.) We celebrated. For the first time in my short-lived life I have felt oddly uneasy with celebrating a Christian holiday. And we have always commemorated St. Nicholas Day and Christmas. But things are different for me now. I have been taking my Bible reading very seriously of late. (My entries attest to this, no doubt. When I re-read my entries I noticed a preacher-like tone! Who would have thought? Would Sytie recognize a changed Margot?)

We should commemorate Passover with relish—don't we have so much in common with our ancient ancestors in Egypt?

Pharaoh's edicts are similar to Hitler's mandate—Jewish numbers should be constrained; Pharaoh vehemently ordered the execution of every first-born male. Is not Hitler executing men and women? Torture, beatings, slaying, public executions. Many Jews are working in labor camps; who knows what their conditions are?

Perhaps they work in a quarry or with cement, like the ancient Hebrews. Perhaps the Germans withhold basic materials just to increase their load and batter their spirits. Which reminds me! Mordechai's speech on the Eve of Passover (I recall nearly every word):

"In God's eye, thousands of years pass before Him like the blink of an eye. Today's history unfolds onto the same fabric of heavenly tapestries; time is immaterial to God. The nuances of our evolutionary story unfold before Him in a heavenly heartbeat.

Do not think for a minute; do not assume for a second, that today's saga is unique to our history. Indeed, we have experienced many hard times before in our long journey through the annals of time.

Remember the bondage in Egypt. You were there.

Remember the bondage of our Babylonian captors. You were there.

Remember the bondage of Persia and of Medea, of Rome. You were there.

Remember the Inquisition. The expulsions. You were there.

Remember the forced enlistments in Russia and the pogroms in Lithuania. You were there.

Remember the blood libels. You were there.

And remember this: You are *still* there.

This Passover Eve you will hold the matzos and recite, "This is the bread of affliction that our forefathers consumed in the land of Egypt." Taste its tastelessness. Taste its blandness.

That is the taste of the Jew before Redemption. Before Exodus.

Taste the bitter herb. Shed the tears of misery. Before Moses split the sea.

Once you taste all the unpleasantness, you will begin to relish the zesty meal.

That is the flavor of God's blessings. His desire to bless all people, especially the ancient Hebrew slaves, with Infinite Goodness. Savor the flavor. For you will need to recall it.

And then, when the recitation of the *Hagadah* is nearly done and over, you again taste the flavor of the matzos' blandness—the unleavened bread of our forefathers. That is the bread of the Jew who must always remember from whence he came. So as to realize where he may fall once again, if he were to fall, as Adam and Eve fell…

But this is not where it all ends.

What do we drink last? We imbibe our fourth and final draft of wine. The sweet essence of richness—the liking to our promise of Final Redemption. Out of nowhere, in a different way, with a different flavor, our Messiah will come and redeem us. He will coax us with words of love; and we will drink with relish the Words of the Lord. After so long the remembrance of bitterness and misery, the final flavor in our mouths will be the essence of Wine and longing.

The fourth and final draft reminds us that although the history of the Jews began on a bitter note, enjoyed fleeting pleasantness, was permeated by bitterness, but will ultimately culminate at last in nothing but savory sweetness.

And we imbibe wine, for wine must undergo a process of fermentation before it can be enjoyed. Are not the Jews in the very process of drastic transformations, like fermented wine before its final tasting?

When will our nation reach its pinnacle? When will we be ready to drink that final draft of wine?

When will God unfold the tapestries of time before His Heavenly Throne and point to a single thread and say, "This is where I will tie the knot. This is where it all ends."

The Silent Sister

We can only pray that next year we shall all join hands in Jerusalem and raise the cup of Elijah… and drink from the cup of Redemption!"

I remember sitting in the room thinking, 'What is the cup of Redemption? How this all sounds so strange! (But how beautiful to contemplate.) Can it truly be that better days are yet to come? How wonderful it is to picture a redeemer, a Messiah. Mordechai's message: is it a harkening of truth or a delusion?'

I do not have answers to those questions. But a flicker of hope remains in my bosom.

Passover Eve was so beautiful and full of meaning that year. We prayed for the Redemption. We hoped the war would end; we prayed for the defeat of our enemies. We desperately wished for the end of all misery.

But alas I am here, in Holland still.

And the war is dragging on.

And Mordechai is somewhere in Europe.

And our cups are empty.

There is no wine.

***

WE HAVE BEEN DISCOVERED. ANNE IS CRYING. MUMMY IS SHORT OF BREATH.
I AM HIDING THIS DIARY IN MY SKIRT.

***

Westerbork, Drenthe
1944

It is so hard to believe, but I feel free. I am finally outside! The air is fresh. I was able to see our chestnut tree in all its fading color after we left our hideaway. Some irises along the path, a violet plum tree and the faintest reminder of blooming rosebushes. A moment of beauty.

And yet all this I am willing to forgo for the hideaway at Westermarkt.

The clogged toilets, the never-ending pea peeling, the squabbles and the frights…

All this I now long for.

I long for the safety of my bed. Even though I was not always comfortable sleeping near my parents, I was safe, far away from the brutal Nazis!

I'll never forget the face of that Gestapo policeman. I recognized him! The death-breath monster. The man who wanted my information, who insisted I write my own death sentence. We later learned the name of that awful commander—Karl Silberbauer. His name was on a plaque by the entrance on Euterpestraat. He deserves no praise.

He licked his lips in glee, pointing his pistol at Daddy and Peter. Enemies of the state, a teacher and a pupil. Jews. Filthy, worthless Jews. His eyes were a very bluish-gray. He was not animated. I could not imagine him smiling or crying. He appeared overtly anxious.

The main Nazi policeman shouted commands at his comrades. They ransacked the *entire* apartment. They were hunting for valuables. Little did they know that most of our 'valuables' were hidden away by M.G. and that the Van Pels sold their precious luxuries long ago.

Anne left her life's work behind. Little did they know the red checkerboard book contained incriminating evidence. They didn't even glance at the myriad papers and paraphernalia. They were too busy searching for gold. A futile quest. All they found was some rubbish in an old tin.

They shuffled Anne's papers; her diary was strewn on the floor. Anne stared at me. 'Should I pick it up?' She seemed to say.

I stared intently back and quietly mouthed, 'No!'

'Why?' she arched her brows in silence.

'Because they'll know it's important if you do!' I thought loudly.

Anne had to pry herself away and muster the self-control of a saint. Her life's work! Garbage in the eyes of the enemy. Tears welled in her eyes. Angry and violated, she hid her face in Mummy's shoulder.

"You have ten minutes!" Rush. Gather your meager things.

I held her hand. We had some packing to do.

We rushed. The shock was more than we could absorb.

This time I knew what was important—a blanket, undergarments, and a sweater. A toothbrush. Socks. And even pens. For you. I needed extra pens for you.

The pushing, the shoving, the crude remarks. And off we went to our 'court of justice,' the Gestapo headquarters. If I can only describe the fear beating in the left chamber of my heart. The pumping of blood, so loud; I feared the discovery of my precious diary and all of its anti-Nazi rhetoric, of its Jewishness, of its very threat to all they stand for, these people who had the power to state "thou shall die" or "thou shall live!" But I did not let anyone know I had safely stored my diary in my long, black skirt. I did not want to endanger anyone.

It may have been foolish, but sometimes foolish acts are brave ones in disguise.

How can I describe on a small piece of paper the cold expression of those policemen?

The fear of slashing, of rape?

The Frank women held hands, and Mrs. Van Pels joined us. Our feminine dignity—will it remain or will they take that away too?

All this crossed our minds...

"Do you know any other Jews in hiding? Where do they live? Who is helping them?"

Sytie. I write this for you. I did not let them know a thing. I did not reveal *any* information. It would be "improper speech." You did not reveal that boy's name that day. And I refuse to state any name. Even if I have to save myself. Thankfully, I did not know anyone in particular. And so I told them I was unaware, and they believed me.

"Do you have any papers that may be incriminating to the Nazi party? Let me make you aware: this is a serious crime!"

I did not reveal my secret diary—you. No. I prepared in advance a hideaway for you, my little book, in an inseam in my skirt. For a day like this, should it arise. Remember what Anne said on that day? Well. Here you are. We are in this together.

"Sir. I do not. I am but an aspiring nurse, Sir."

He snickered and glanced at his friend. "Nurse! Well, you'll gain a great deal of experience where you're going. I can promise you that!"

He shut his book. With force, in my face.

He pointed to Anne.

"What's your name?"

Anne was not afraid of the bulldog.

"Anne Frank. I was born in Germany. And I am fifteen!"

They laughed her off.

"Jewish pride. And arrogance! So, fifteen-year-old girl, what do *you* aspire to?"

"I want to be a Hollywood star!"

Both of them gawked. Anne protected herself. She did not want them to know—that yes—she has all of that incriminating evidence. In the Annexe! And so help us God, the Dutch will know what happened. The world will know who is the Nazi and what is this senselessness, this utter madness.

Mummy and Anne were distraught beyond measure when Karl Silberbauer bellowed questions at Daddy. But Daddy remained strong and did not show any fear...They wanted to know if we knew of other fellow Jews in hiding. Of course we didn't, but liars never believe the truth when they hear it.

(To add to it all, I began menstruating. Luckily, I did not forget to bring sanitary napkins with me. I wasn't expecting it today, but terror brought my menses two days in advance.)

They drove us off to Huis van Bewaring, on the Weteringschans. A prison!

Our crime: resisting deportation!

Together with rapists, thieves, pimps, and even murderers, we, the Frank sisters did keep company. By the peaceful canal waters we looked out from our prison cells aghast.

What have we done wrong?

How often have I *nearly* passed by this area as a young girl, but Mummy surely did not permit me?

Mummy would say, "Margot. Turn your bicycle, dearest. Come around *this* way!" She would apprehensively point to the North.

And I would ask, "Why Mummy? I want to go that way." I would point toward the Weteringschans.

"Sweetheart. That is a dangerous place. Bad people go there! Please, listen to Mummy."

And off I would pedal toward Mummy.

(Mummy's fears have a way of coming to pass.

Please Mummy, stop fearing if this is what is to come!)

The prison is filthy.

Anne and I slept on the same cot. We all shared the same cell. Mrs. Van Pels cried the entire night. Of course there were no handkerchiefs. She used her skirt to wipe her tears.

"What has become of Augusta? What has become of me?"

The cell was crammed with homeless, toothless, and dirty women.

I recognized an old lady. She is the beggar I all-too often saw in the hospital, 'sick' with the flu or 'dehydrated.' The hospital staff found innovative ways to keep her off the streets and astutely diagnosed her with random illnesses. On certain occasions, especially when the weather was either too hot or too cold, they provided her with an alias and concluded she had "bed sores." She remained in the hospital for further care.

When the situation was really terrible, such as the outbreak of the flu a few months before we went into hiding, rumor has it she dressed as one of the nurses just to remain in the building!

She did not recognize me.

I stared at her for a long time that night.

∗∗

Off to the train platform. And now in Westerbork. Drenthe. Mordechai's refugee home. And now mine.

"The breeding ground for illegitimate children." M.G. said this. Remember?

Diary, Diary. Dear Diary. What has become of us?

This 'transit' camp is the home of a people who are without a home. A people without a country; our wanderings have led us here. Destination—Westerbork, Holland. An ugly and ill-kempt place. They bolted the doors behind us. And I turned around and saw nothing but a wall, painted with dull-green varnish.

Daddy says this place looks "hopeful" and that "conditions are not as bad as I thought." But there are few amenities here! And the mud is everywhere. It is as if the Dutch military patrol and the regular policemen never bothered to pave the ground here the same way no one bothers to fix a house before moving into another one. Tis a resting stop.

And we are prisoners here too.

Assigned to barracks 67. The Punishment Block. Block S.

We are inmates convicted of a crime: failure to report for deportation.

Most of the people who came here in the past are no longer here. They have been exiled to "relocation in the East," banished.

'Relocation'. A euphemism. We know what it means. But we dare not speak a word. We've heard enough from the BBC to know precisely what the "East" means for people branded with a 'J'.

It is not yet autumn, our beds of brick and our straw mattresses, if we can call them that, offer little warmth.

Here we will lie our heads down at night and pray for English and American soldiers to bash German heads with bullets and with bombs. One! Two! Three! Come on! And Hurry! Blast the brains of Nazis if you must…but get here! Come. Fast.

I am with Mummy now, and with Anne. Nothing here belongs to us. We are waiting for someone or something to tell us,

'You can go now. You can go back to your homes. The war is over. Hitler is dead. The Germans are dead. The machine guns don't work anymore. The tanks are tired, and the soldiers returned to their mothers' homes. You can cook your meals and buy your bread. Come on. Get up now. Pick up that heavy head. No, I am not joking around with you. No, I am not a good dream. Yes, this is real.'

Anne is in a frenzy. She can't believe I smuggled this in.

We relinquished our clothes when we arrived. My skirt had the inseam, and my diary was in the skirt. They wanted my skirt for storage. They plan on returning my clothes when I'll be called for deportation to the East. When I realized this, I told the guard I forgot my "feminine hygiene product" in my skirt pocket. I then handed him a Dutch coin. "Please, may I retrieve it?" He looked me over. He said, "Hurry!" And hurry I did. He showed me the room where the clothes of the latest 'shipment of personnel' were stored. After a quick prayer and a hurried search, I found you, hidden away. You were still warm from the heat of my thigh.

My prisoner's outfit has pockets—and now an in-seamed pocket too. I showed the guard my booty— pre-placed sanitary napkins. I handed him another coin.

Yes, Anne. I have my diary with me. And no. I am not crazy. This is what keeps me sane.

***

Batteries. We are taking apart old airplane batteries and cleaning them, repairing them.

How ironic—we are *aiding* our enemies!

The musty odor is slightly reminiscent of urine-stained wooden planks so often 'sniffed' on late summer evenings. Usually, one can escape the unpleasant odor by hurrying past its source. Here—the entire block is infested with this odor, and there is no breeze by the canals to carry it out to sea.

Batteries. Rotted electrical poles, once capable of transmitting electrical energy now stain our fingertips with a neon-copper hue. I suspect their toxicity is dangerous, so Anne and I decided to hold our breath each time we discard the batteries. The room is filled with dusty particles, and sometimes I can even taste copper and nickel in my mouth. It tastes like congealed blood and rusty nails.

Batteries. Breaking apart and replacing tarnished ones…

"This is worse than peas!" Anne finally forces a smile on Mummy's zombie-like expression, transforming her for a moment. A glimpse. A figment of what once was.

"At least we could cook and eat them," I murmured.

"And my nails would still look pretty after I washed them…" Mrs. Van Pels added.

"And don't forget, after a while we finished peeling them!" Mummy finally croaked. She has been ever-so-silent since we arrived.

We've been hungrier since the Gestapo shipped us all here. I have lost my appetite on occasion, though. The urine-stench back 'home' (the 'block') helps suppress the urge to consume anything.

The Batteries. Piles upon piles.

Stacked upon each other.

In disarray. Airplane batteries, transmitters, and adaptors—all strewn in a large bin, tangled and shapeless.

What is it about piles and piles of anything really that churns one's stomach?

So, when I go to work, I lose the other half of my appetite, and I am no longer so hungry.

Pim visited tonight. He makes an effort to visit us girls every night. We are separated from the men now. Anne is strolling with Peter. Many ladies ask me if I am Anne's sister. "They make such a lovely pair…" Yes… they do…

"Do you have a beau? "Are you the elder?" and so forth. I have my own inquiries. "Do you know a Mordechai Kotsk?" Most simply frown and shake their heads. Back and forth. Back and forth. Some women stare at me. I repeat my question in German. No luck.

We are a displaced people; strangers.

A woman sleeping adjacent to me is staring at me now. She has three separate rings underneath each eye. The right eye suffers from a constant twitch of which she is wholly unaware.

Another woman is fond of Mozart's *Don Juan* and seems rather hard of hearing. She sleeps to my left.

Across from my bed, which I share with Anne, a pregnant woman rubs her belly and another begs for some cloth to absorb her menses.

I gaze at the floor beneath me. Its grayish color is reminiscent of the backstreets off of Rembrandtplein.

I close my eyes. My private space is within me. I walk outdoors. I try to breathe cool air. (Momentary reprieves.)

There is a long line of women waiting their turn for the W.C.

No one touches or leans on the walls because they are stained with feces.

At least ten women wait their turn. Even late at night.

The lavatories are mostly clogged, and all different types of 'human calls of nature' are on display for the viewer's discontent.

Children wail incessantly. Their mothers do not have food to satisfy their aching bellies. One little boy walks aimlessly by, his dirty diaper hanging heavily between his knees. He runs around, cries, sucks his thumb and whines for hours on end. I take him to the W.C. I cleaned his clothes. It turns out he belongs in the orphanage block. His name is Levi, and he doesn't know when his mommy is coming back.

I think of baby Gaby and cry. Where is her mommy?

Most of the children in Westerbork don't have parents.

Can there be blessings in such a place?

Indeed, I still have Mummy and Pim!

This block house is like a stationary train ride, where every passenger keeps to herself, extending one's boundaries, uncomfortable with the formidable "EYE STARE;" we are all evading one another here. But we keep staring at each other, as if the other person has some interesting story to tell, which she won't share but we can't help but wonder what it may be.

At this rate, we will soon receive diplomas in our area of expertise: voyeurism.

One can hardly be blamed.

***

I believe God paves our roads and marks our paths with precision.

Mrs. Steiner, the lady who rubs her belly across from me, began pacing the block at approximately 1:45 am last night, stopping every fifteen minutes to breathe deeply and squat. After two hours of this stop and go movement, she fell to the floor on her buttocks, with knees and legs extended forward. Arching her back, she yelled, "Please! Is there a doctor here? Please! Someone, help me!"

4:15 am. The block stirred. Yet no one went to her aid. Women were afraid to get involved…

There are no doctors here.

Mrs. Steiner's groans, her cries of agony, left every woman awake in her bed that night. We were baffled. What should we do?

A woman's head appeared from the right. "Push!"

Another woman insisted, "Wait until you feel a contraction!"

"Squat!"

"Don't sit on the floor! Go to a bed!"

An older woman with a cane came to her aid. She walked slowly over from my side of the room. She wore a kerchief on her head and was nearly hunchbacked. She removed her head cover and placed it on the woman's head. She tucked in any loose strands of hair. She told the young woman to remain focused. She patted her head again and again. Shh…. she kept whispering. The older woman provided the warmth of a doula …

"Push!" She whispered. "Squeeze my hand if it hurts you." Soon, another woman joined and patted her head with compresses.

I ran to the group.

"I'm Margot Frank. What's your name?"

In an inaudible voice, the birthing mother said, "Vera Steiner."

"Mrs. Steiner, can I feel your baby's head?"

"Are you a midwife? A nurse? You look young."

"I am young. But I volunteered at a hospital. I think I might be able to help you," I said as reassuringly as possible.

She nodded her head and closed her eyes.

Mrs. Steiner consented.

I rushed outside (the toilets are there) and washed my hands with whatever remaining soap I could find, careful to not touch any dirty surface. I bumped into the feces-stained walls—it was so dark outside! I ran to the bathroom a second time and slowed down a bit.

137

I quickly assembled a makeshift delivery room.

"I need alcohol! I need a needle! I need scissors! If you have these items, please lend them to me!" I yelled these instructions, to the chagrin of a few sleeping women.

One religious woman gave me a pair of scissors. Another cloth. One woman gave me a blanket. Another a pacifier. One woman handed me a baby's hat. "This is all we have."

I began to pray. "Please God. Help this woman. We need alcohol. Please!"

I ran to Mrs. Steiner's side. "Please! Come here! I feel something!" she cried.

I inserted my hand gently into her canal and continued until I felt the baby's head. Sure enough, I felt the baby's head in ready position. As I checked once more, I realized his neck needed a bit of shifting downward. I very gently felt for the baby's nose and slowly pushed his head a bit downwards. The mother screamed as I did this.

"Ooh! I need to push now!"

"Wait for a contraction!" The old lady exhorted.

Vera Steiner waited a half-second and began pushing. The baby's head began to peek through.

"Push!" Some of the women in the room began to cheer.

"I can see his head!" one woman yelled.

"That's not his head! That's the bulge of her body!" her friend retorted.

Out of excitement, Mrs. Steiner began pushing again.

"NO! Do not push like that, Mrs. Steiner. You're wasting your energy. Use your abdominal muscles, not your face! You're turning blue!" I told her.

"I feel something… Is that the baby?" Vera asked.

I said no and bellowed, "Quickly! Someone! Get me paper or cloth. She's had a bowel movement!"

"Oh my!" Embarrassed, Vera began to weep.

The old lady reassured her that many women have this experience.

I asked a kind lady (who later introduced herself as Rachel Horowitz) to wipe away the feces. "I hope you don't mind. I don't want to risk contaminating the mother's vaginal canal or the baby. I need to keep my hands clean…"

"No problem! I am glad to help…"

My mother and Anne stood near me. Anne held her hand to her mouth.

And then, the baby's hair, so black and his head so red, peeked through the maternal fortress.

"I see the baby! I see him!"

"How do you know it's a him? Maybe it's a her?"

Mrs. Steiner gained energy from the room.

"Yes, Mrs. Steiner!" I told her. "Just a little more!"

She pushed more and more.

Vera began to smile and wince at the same time. The room was silent. Even the littlest ones dared not stir. With a wail unlike any other I've heard since that day in the hospital back in Amsterdam and long before this journey into Westerbork, Mrs. Steiner expelled her newborn daughter with the agonizing cry of a lone mother churning the crucible of electrifying pain. Her vagina reverberated, her thighs shook, her knees held tightly by two makeshift doulas; the mother groaned together with her newborn's first cry of life. The crowd now cheered, and Mrs. Steiner's baby was enveloped in a white bed sheet, sprinkled with water, although still bloodied. With the umbilical cord still attached, the baby cried for its mother's nipples and her soothing voice.

"One more push!" and the fetus's life source gushed; a mass of congealed blood, purple and blue, veined and marked with blood. No longer necessary, no longer the source of life's sustenance.

"I found this." A strange woman said.

My alcohol. A woman gave me some vodka.

I disinfected the scissors. My hands too. I used the needle to close the tear to her perineum.

All was going well. The vodka giver disappeared…

I quickly knotted the cord and discarded the placenta.

Mrs. Steiner held my hand and pulled me close, to her ears—

"God bless you! She is just as much my daughter as she is yours."

She mouthed the words, 'Thank You.'

Anne ran to me and hugged me.

"Margot! I *never* knew you could do that! You were born to do this! You were wonderful!"

She said aloud to the room, "This is my sister!"

Many of the women retired to their beds, exhausted.

The exact time of little Steiner's birth: 5:59 am.

God Himself in His Glory guided my hand. Just as he guided the hand of Pharaoh's maidservant toward Moses's tar-basket floating in the crocodile infested waters of the river Nile.

God maneuvered my hands that night.

And the baby swam toward and into my hands.

The waters did not drown the baby; and the baby drank from the bounty of her mother's breast in peace and in utter serenity that night.

***

Westerbork is a strange place. Blocks of rectangular buildings dot the camp with little aesthetic touches; they do not appeal to one's pleasure in nature, its flora and fauna. The camp has been in use for some years now. Mordechai's family may have bunked in my block… the paint on the walls has long tarnished. And the rotting smell of wood envelops the camp, especially the women's section. No one knows why.

It is cold in the evenings. My warm duvet cover back in my lovely Amsterdam bedroom suddenly comes to mind. I wonder if a stranger is sleeping in my bed tonight. Oddly, I am not fantasizing over our Back House. I never really considered that place a home. Only a hideaway.

Few here have the necessary skill to replace the wretched batteries—but we've all become experts overnight.

My mind is dulled by the monotony of repetition.

Vera Steiner's baby is not sleeping well at night. We are all sleep-deprived women, without sharing the comfort of a newborn. Many of us young women wonder if we will die with our virginity intact. We wonder if our wombs will fill with nourishing fluids and a wondrous baby.

I overheard one of the girls whisper to her friend, "Let's just do it now before it's too late."

Girls my age want a chance to make love before the Nazis get a chance at making their lives a living hell. Stories of utter Gehenna surface, enough to tempt a timid girl into the arms of an all-too-willing gentleman eager to pass along his life force.

I wonder if Mordechai would try to tempt me if he were here now. And I wonder if I would succumb to his temptation.

Would he adhere to his Orthodox upbringing and refrain from touching or kissing me?

I never dipped in the holy waters of the *mikvah* after all! And I would not have had occasion to be wooed, much less betrothed.

Is it such a cruel and evil act, to make love, when there is so little love to make out in this place?

How I do wonder what it may feel like…to be lost for one moment… to feel the pull of my mortality…and the push of my immortality.

And would he love me, at all?

***

Rumors die and rumors are born.
Rumors of trainloads of corpses and
Rumors of our enemy's defeat.
'Did you hear of this story?'
And 'Did you hear that?'
Ruth was raped.
Sarah was found in the men's camp last night. Drunk.
The men have more broth.
The toilets are clogged.
The stories border on the absurd, too.
Some women become pregnant from the poisoned water.
Oh, and did you hear?
The British are controlling parts of Northern Holland
and the Germans, frightened, ran away like a bunch of elephants.
We always knew they were scared of mice-the Jewish menace.

The latest circulating bits of information are cruelly transmitted:
Did you know that soon the Nazis will close down Westerbork and build a school here instead?
And, such as they are born, they die.
Sarah was sleeping the whole night it seems. In a different cot.

Ruth slept with her husband.
The men share their broth.
And the toilets are still clogged.
We welcome good news, but the "news" is too "fantastic":
Eisenhower decimated enemy battalions overnight.
The Americans devised a secret weapon to wipe out every German.
The Nazi party is defunct. Hitler's henchmen turned against him.
[A coup d'état?]
and the Jews are no longer the supreme enemy. The homosexuals and
the Poles are.
Becoming adept at splitting hairs
is my newest mission.
And my latest goal:
to remain with a few tufts of hair.

***

Too edgy to speak with anyone and too tired to go for a walk I stare
at the ceiling.
There are no answers there.
Twisting and turning at night, I stare at the walls.
There are no answers there.
Tears flow
For the relentless mystery of our future.
Too much evil in the world.
I search my soul for the strength of the world.
Perhaps there are some answers there.
Margot. This may be the beginning
Of the end or the end of many beginnings.
You are not in control.
The world rotates on its
axis, the sun firmly
sits in the firmament,
and the trainloads
continue to chug to
their final destination.
You do not stir the stars

The Silent Sister

nor do you know the vast
intricacies of their lifespan
and eventual death.
You are but a bystander.
The sun rises today.
It will set tomorrow.
The wheels go round and round—
You are not in control.
Did you every cry because you
could not command the
moon to shine on the day
it cruelly hid from you?
Dark and Cold.
Your life is barely your own.
You stand still, while
a world of joy and grace spins around you.
You stand still.
Yet, you are always moving.
And you cannot say
"To this, I will say 'STOP'"
and "To this I will say – 'Go!'"
God alone retains the power over the cosmos.
He holds the steering wheel.
Yet never does He boast;
He never demands
The attention He so rightfully deserves.

To the one who
set into motion
the playground of the universe
Sit, ask, and pray.
Tears, if they must flow,
(for they certainly tend to)
must flow from a
place of awe and wonder
and not from fear.

So, Margot, I tell
you tonight—
Fear not for your
Soul, for you are
Innocent, holy, and pure.
Fear for the Day of Judgment
For Evil will never cry, "Victory!"

My soul's trip around the world
This time around may prove
Yet to be the end of a long-awaited journey,
The middle of a final destination or perhaps the beginning of a long crusade.
Know a higher power
Has set this world into motion
And He can, at will,
Command it to end.
Or,
Perhaps God will return the world to the initial moments of Utter Perfection,
The first day of Mankind's long sojourn in this world,
Perhaps He will spin the universe in reverse
And all Evil will
Consume itself
As the Earth rotates
Backwards
And all that will remain is the One God who said,
"Let there be Light."
And to all those who have retained their inner Light pure, holy, and innocent, to
Them God shall say,
"Bask in My Eternal Glory."
And there will be light.

***

The cobblestone roads of Amsterdam's canal streets are etched upon my memory. Twice a day, especially on Sundays, a man in a checkered suit would clean the streets for the church-goers and the many visitors and shoppers on the Westermarkt. The aroma of coffee brewing by the Brewster's stall... the myriad cheeses on display... the buttery biscuits... the pancakes with vanilla 'buttons'... all this inflicts painful nostalgia. There are no luxuries in Westerbork. There's no one but us to clean our bunks and beds here.

The street vendors. I remember the fat lady trying to sell the mussels. She did have the dirtiest apron in our part of town! I wonder if Fat Son is still trying to start up with his mother. Her ladle is probably broken by now...

Anne and I have been trying to get our hands on some Belgian chocolates. A few of the refugees have been bartering their goods in exchange for other much-needed pharmaceuticals. The Belgian women need feminine hygiene products, but so do we! So much for chocolate. We didn't have much in our luggage to entice buyers. Perhaps I'll hand over some precious paper in exchange for a little caramel and nougat-covered chocolate. One can't be too sentimental here.

***

My neighbors have a rendezvous tomorrow night with two gentlemen! Again, I am overhearing other people's conversations. It seems one girl, probably Anne's age, will meet her 'boyfriend' for a walk. They plan on getting 'lost' in a designated area, pre-prepared with a bed and a pillow.... The other couple will meet a couple of hours later and make use of the same room later on in the evening. All this is going on in the midst of terrible warnings of horrendous death-threats. Why do people become even more passionate when war becomes a part of the equation?

Henrietta! Goodness knows where she is now. Perhaps she is in hiding like Jetteke. Either way, Henrietta made love with one of her suitors... many girls and boys are thinking just as she did it seems. What did she say? "I want to do it before I die."

Perhaps they want to know what life is all about before the time comes and they won't be able to discover *much* about life.

So much for waiting for the best moments in life to experience life fully.

Sometimes people stub themselves in the foot.

And sometimes life stabs people in the heart.

***

Fear of transports! If only we can last out the war! It seems this war is dragging on into eternity. Each day that passes lends us one extra night to breathe and an extra day to wonder—will this be the day that I die? Will this be the day I am sent off to the East!?

We've made some new friends here. Rachel is older than Anne and me by ten years or more. She is a very patient and kind listener. Although I do not have much contact with the women here, I have come to notice that many women try to make the most of the situation in Westerbork. Rachel is eager to remain here for as long as possible. "Transport is just the most terrible reality of this place. We all know what the destiny is of all those people on the trains…and to give them back their clothes! For what?"

She is heartbroken over the tragic truth of this place—that those who leave are never seen again. For some reason, the prisoners of Westerbork receive their clothes, which they relinquished when they arrived, upon departure. (Abraham van Witsen is the supervisor.) But who knows what the Germans plan to do with the clothes once they arrive at their final destination? Every Monday the terrible Germans and their eager Dutch cronies check off names on a list for deportation and transport. Every Tuesday a thousand prisoners depart Westerbork.

Mummy and I fear we shall be called. If so, we are more than likely to be sent off to some distant destination where horrors await us, as the rumors go… Poland. "The East."

We shake with fear to think that soon our names will be on the LIST. Anne remains optimistic because Daddy seems optimistic too. "Soon the war will be over. There are rumors Paris fell to the Allies." It is hard to know what is truth and what is far from truth.

I can only live in the present. And for now, my hands are shaking! Pray for the best locket diary.

***

News from the IPA! The Israelite Press Agency announced the approach of the Russians, and the English have almost reached Arnhem! Are these rumors? Who knows! There are rumors there won't be another transport! Rachel thinks the rumors may be true, but she doesn't know. I agree with her. I am optimistic. Maybe we'll stay here until we are liberated! Lights out.

***

I write in my diary in the bathroom. I don't want anyone to know I have this with me. I try to clean the stall as well as I can, and then I write. It is hard for me to concentrate, especially today, because the stalls are so dirty and wretchedly smelly. I wish I had a switch to turn my nose off...

We've come a long way, us Franks. We are ever so committed and close now that we are struggling to survive in this hellish world. Anne and Mummy don't bicker all that much anymore. Anne and I are as close as we could have wished. We hold hands occasionally, especially when we hear bad news. It is as if we are five or six again.

Holland has been a hospitable home for us. Germany was my homeland; my birthplace. But then Germany became a dirty word, and we moved to Holland as refugees. We thought it would end there; we believed our home on the Merwedeplein would serve as our safety net from the German warlords. And now, after hiding like dirty rats in a meat factory, we've come out to play in the backstreets of Northern Holland. Westerbork.

God! How I thought this place would remain a piece of information, a place I heard of, a place somehow connected to a man I once knew, Mordechai. I thought it would end there. How it has become my home!

The Dutch police corps runs this place, in lieu of the German Gestapo. It seems wherever one goes on this continent, he will find a Nazi sympathizer. A Nazi lover.

Comrades in pretty boots and with hateful expressions. They don't mind the "job" of "assisting the oppressors."

Mordechai was right—the Jew is dirty in the eyes of the German/Dutch loving Nazis.

How else can people treat others this way? First, they must deem them "dirty" and "inhuman" so they can them treat them inhumanely. And it is justified to call young women criminals if they resist deportation to their proper destination—the East. Poland.

Rachel and the girls don't talk too much about their fears. Instead, we talk about life before the war and—FOOD.

This is fine. I like to fantasize about *oliebolletje* too.

But, like Mummy, I have this deep-seated fear about the future.

I'm afraid I won't have much of one.

***

It's Friday night and I am sitting in the bathroom stall crying. I miss dinners by the Goslars! Hanneli. Where is she now!? Mr. Goslar would recite the blessings on the wine and the bread. During the cold winter months Mrs. Goslar prepared the matzo-ball soup. Where are they now?

They hate us for being Jews—and we had so little Jewishness in our lives!

The Goslars helped me connect with God. Mummy and I would attend synagogue; on Yom Kippur we would praise God for His thirteen attributes of mercy: "Merciful, Compassionate…" I would sit in the synagogue and wonder how a man such as Moses could speak to God. My pangs of hunger would momentarily disappear when I bowed my head in submission. The cantor would rail, *"El, Rachoum, VeChanoun…"* Hebrew words of a time long past.

On the Feast of Tabernacles, "Sukkoth," we would chase each other between the yards on Merwedeplein and the Zuideramstellaan. The makeshift tent rattled in the breeze toward the evening. Mummy prepared sweet pastries. Anne almost choked from mirth and giddiness one year. Where is that laughter now?

Baby Gaby.

She was the closest thing to a baby sister…bathing her on Sundays… taking her for walks.

Is she an orphan now? How my heart aches for little Gabriella!

Pause. Tears. Wipe. On sleeve.

I want a baby so badly! I want to hold a baby! I want to nurse a baby and sing to a baby and bathe a baby and cuddle a baby and tickle a baby and stroll with a baby and kiss a baby! Before my conception and birth, before descending to this world, You surely set out a goal and a purpose for me. Will I become a mother or will I be deprived of my dreams?

(Baby Gabriella—is she in Your arms now, like so many children, or is Hanneli holding her hand?)

It is so very hard to keep one's faith here, but there are Orthodox women who pray every day and recite Psalms. I watch them and silently emulate their ways.

"God is merciful; it is mankind who is cruel."

"God destroyed Sodom and Gomorrah, who knows what God will do to the Nazis."

"Have faith. Look at these brutal Nazis—they have the face of bulldogs. Who knows what their souls look like? Look at yourself—you may be a victim of persecution, but evil spirits and evil thoughts are not persecuting you."

I overhear the women on Friday evenings, asking when "candle lighting" begins, so they may pray. "Come Sabbath, come the Bride of the Week." They have no challah and beautiful candelabra to greet the Sabbath with—instead, they greet the Queen of the week with their souls and holy words. They sing. They praise God. "God will have mercy and vindicate the Jewish people."

Sadly, many Orthodox women cannot have physical contact with their husbands because there is no proper *mikvah* in Westerbork. They are considered *niddah*—the menstruate woman. The husbands and wives are committed to God more than they are committed to their personal needs. They look at one another with longing and with burning desire, but they do not dare touch one another—as God does not allow a Jewish man to touch a menstruate woman—a ritually impure woman cannot share a man's bed nor may a man have physical contact with such a woman.

Sytie. You taught me these laws. Remember? Where are you now?

Did the Nazis shatter your life too?

You, who have demonstrated such kindness to a stranger, to a boy who was impulsive and rude, you— should you become the victim of propaganda and slander?

But you are so very careful not to speak ill of any individual!

Little do they care who little understand what caring is…

Sytie, I think of you tonight.

And I think of Baby Gaby tonight.

And I whisper a silent prayer in the chambers of my heart.

God. Please watch over these lovely people, as a shepherd boy watches over his sheep.

***

We were called for transport!

Pim is running around frantically begging for help. He thinks he can get us all transferred to Theresienstadt. Everyone is hoping for a postponement. Janny and her sister are called too! Papa waited for nearly five hours this morning. He spoke with the officers, begged them…Please! Theresienstadt… not the East. Not the blasted East… He is unwilling to give up. "Liberation in the Netherlands is days away," Papa says. He wants us to stay in Westerbork. "The war will end any day now. I know it!" It is hard to know for sure if he will succeed. I have to go. Someone is knocking on my door. "It's urgent!" Someone needs to use this place for what it was intended for. Bye now.

***

We are to go then. Mummy is crying. She cannot shake off her fear. "What will be? What will be?" Daddy is consoling her. And I am saying good bye to you. I do not know what use I will have for you. I'm going off to the East, after all. You are a small miracle—you certainly should have been left behind long ago. But I will keep you in my secret inseam pocket for as long as I can. If you become a danger to me or to my family, I will either dispose of you or burn you or get rid of you as I deem fit. I know this is neither kind nor customary. You are my loyal confidante. But these are dire days.

You have served me well, Diary.

Although I wished to confide in you my secrets and my grandest desires, it seems I have mostly cried on your pages or pondered away…

I would have liked for my granddaughter to read your little secrets. It seems you and I have the only keys, and only you and I know of its contents.

Forgive me. In you go now. Hide away from the world.

Auschwitz
1944

I am in utter Hell. But I found a piece of heaven too.

My daddy is so far away from me. He is with the men. On the other side.

The dead are piled high by the train rails.

Off the ghastly trains a prisoner did greet us.

"Say you are strong." "You are capable."

He did guide my hand. In this inferno. A momentary companion.

"Margot?! Is that you?"

I could not breathe. No food for three days. A ghost. From the desert.

Why are you in striped pajamas? Tears flow.

"Margot!"

"Mordechai?"

He nodded. Tears down his eyes. Mordechai failed. He is here too.

And then he said,

"I am sorry Margot. I let you down. They captured me. I am a prisoner too."

I could not speak. He continued.

"To live you must lie. Tell Anne to say she's sixteen!"

"Keep your shoes. Do not share your socks. Stay with your mother! Margot!"

In a rush of screams and truncheons from the left and right comes the sound of a voice from a faraway town, my Amsterdam.

Mordechai shares the whips and the barks. He marches with me, ere he must depart.

His eyes are sunken. He is a Mussulman. His index finger and his left thumb are chopped off. One ear is missing. And he has three teeth.

I am lost. "Margot. My darling…" Mordechai paves the way for me.

I summon my voice.

"Mordechai. Where are we?"

His eyes swell. "Margot. You're in Auschwitz. But you can live if you stay strong and avoid the selections."

"There's no time to explain Margot. Follow your mother. Stay with Anne!"

"Mordechai! Where are we going? Where is my father going? Papa!"

"Listen to me. Your father is going to be with the men."

I turn my back. I bellow. "Papa!"

Mordechai pulls me away. I receive a blow on my shoulder.

"PAPA!"

"Margot! If you live through this war—I will meet you again by Westermarkt. I promise. By the shul. We will see each other again—promise me!"

I could not speak. The black night penetrated my mind.

Mordechai insisted. He stopped me. He held my shoulders.

"I promise you my heart." He said.

My tongue remained stuck to my mouth. My heart ached and my legs shivered.

I stood in Auschwitz and heard a promise.

"My soul has made love to you a long time ago, Margot." He whispered in my ear.

And he fell to the ground. A dog grabbed his knee. Blood soaked his pants.

Nazi guards whisked him away.

Forever.

He passed the gate he should not have passed to promise me his love.

"Margot! Westermarkt! SWEAR!" He screamed.

"Margot! Palestine! Margot! Palestine!" He repeated.

"Shut up you f----ng Jew!" The Nazis did not like to hear his words.

I did not swear. I held my hand to my mouth.

"I promise, Mordechai." I whispered.

The moon's light disappeared.

Margot did hear a dog bark and she did hear a gunshot amidst the uproar.

Margot thinks Mordechai did not die.

Because if Mordechai dies Margot will surely follow.

***

They buzzed my pubic hair, and I have no mane. Margot is a *blode Kuhe* and *Untermenschen*.

Vera Steiner held her newborn. She was holding onto her death sentence.

All the kinderlach were gassed. The orphans joined their parents.

I hope the reunion was lovely.

We saw them march. They were enthusiastic. Maybe they thought they would get a nice treat after their showers.

Anne lied. She is 'sixteen' now. The doctor with the white coat and the eyes the color of a Siberian Tiger commanded her to stand to the right. With a grin. As if he knew her secret.

We are together still. Mummy. Anne. Margot.

Anne lied to live.

The gas chambers are in full operation. The smog and unmistakable scent of burning flesh permeate the camps. It's too bad the children could not sprout a couple of good inches overnight. Perhaps the doctor would have sent them to our barracks if they did.

All that remains of them is the stench in my nostrils.

***

I cannot see, for my glasses are forever lost in a heap of gnarled spectacles. Clear vision: only two inches from my nose. I am like a lost child in a crowded train station. The world appears as but a shadow, as if my eyes are relentlessly drenched with tears. All is a blur.

But I hear their boots. And I smell the burning flesh. It unremittingly permeates the camp. And I wonder if I will disappear like all those poor orphans. Into thin air.

***

They bark at us. At three in the morning. *Shnell*! We must stand in the cold mist until the sun decides to come up. Girls collapse. We are naked. My breasts are on full display. The guards mock and deride us. We are 'filthy Jews'. Some point. Some snicker. Most don't flinch. We are not women. We are mice.

Our toes are frost-bitten. Our bodies shiver until we become numb. The Germans smile. They wear fur-lined coats and tall leather boots. They take great pleasure in witnessing our pain.

Filth. They call us Jewish filth. Our teeth are black. Our fingernails are dirty.

But we share what we have.

Anne and I share our soup ration. We sip the bowl. We pass the brackish soup to our friends and to Mummy. If we find a potato we consider ourselves very rich.

If our ration of margarine is missing we consider ourselves paupers.

Today I am rich. I drank an extra sip of soup. Anne wants to "pamper" me today.

Anne distributes the bread ration. She is very fair. No one complains because she is kind. She is crying now because she lost her ration, even though she gave everyone a fair portion.

***

Margot is going to hide this diary near the shithole where the Nazi guards never bother to check because the rancidness is more distasteful than killing Jews.

The first time I hid you in my shoe. The ugly clog. (I kept you safe while I was stamped with a tattoo number. 989345. It is still red.)

I eat from my clog and drink from it too. A Pole stole my soup bowl and a Greek woman my spoon. I am very poor. The rich girls have a knife and a few strands of hay.

Mummy never taught me how to steal and how to lie and how to shove and how to push and how to hurt and how to scream my way about.

We Dutch are a different brand. These girls have been here for a long time.

Wait—
What did you say?
You don't want me to bury you!?
I need to bury you away because my naked body is for all to see.
I am a specimen. But I have no pocket on my skin.
This place is a laboratory. But I will disinter you if I can. I won't forget you!

Anne and I don't want to be alone. We want to be with Mummy.
We are afraid of the dark.
And we do not want to see the dead people on the floor anymore.
If we are with Mummy maybe we can drink some milk.
Mummy says it's nice to share milk with your little sister.

***

The Day of Atonement is here. I pray God is merciful. I see a *Kapo*!

***

I need to bury you for good. But I can't just yet. Be patient.
I have only ten pages left in my locket diary. You have been unfair to me. When I need you—you run away from me?
Just like Mordechai. And where is Daddy? Mummy needs Daddy too.
Anne says I am still beautiful.
But I am bleeding on my scalp today, and I forgot to wash my head.

***

Anne is in the Kratzeblock. Scabies! She cannot die alone. I am going to Anne.

***

Mummy wants me to stay with her. I want to stay with her too, but who will stay with Anne? Lenie and Mummy dug a tunnel under the wood. Our stomach ached more than our skin itched. Now my Mummy gave me bread for Anne. Anne must live. She is life. We shared bread. I gave her most of the bread. She needs me. I don't care if I die.

Outside the soil provides standing water every day.

There are no birds here. Not a fly. The sky is never blue.

I thought I saw vultures on the dead heads though.

This is Auschwitz.

***

The hungry dogs bark at every hour. The Nazis make sure they have a hearty appetite—so we Jews can satisfy them. We serve as prey.

There is plenty of food here—for worms and for rats. Their world is fertile. The supply of nurturing food is ongoing. Meals and snack time are provided. The fleas are certainly in Paradise and the lice are doubly rewarded each day. The living quench their thirst, and the dead encourage their desire for more living flesh.

There are no souls here. No one sings. There are only bitter tears and the screeches of the mad and the diseased.

The Kratzeblock is a haven for bugs eager to suck our bodies dry. Perhaps the bugs sing a wonderful song as they fill their empty bellies with blood.

The silence of a dead horizon promises no rainbow's end and rewards no respite.

There are no more children.

Screeches, brawls, violence outbreaks. Fights in feces and mud in one's mouth. Kapos relish the right to clobber.

And the thieves relish their sweet breads.

Stolen today—in the latrines the bread ends up tomorrow.

The goo of what once was bread now yellow, sandy, and smashed, moistens the corpses piled near the latrine's exit.

The snow then covers the remnants of that bread—the sustenance of the humans here on Earth.

***

I am only eighteen; I dreamed of a life within my own. My womb is desiccated now. No menstrual flow reminds me of womanhood. Only a few tears are left for my unborn children. My baby son's breath. My little daughter's hands. They too are gone.

The winter months are bitter. It is as if my bones are frozen and will never thaw. My flesh shivers to warm my body, but my skin does not warm in response. This bitterness is causing such fatigue. I want to scream from exhaustion and misery. Mummy tries to warm me with her pats, but her hands are *so* cold. Anne still needs me, and we fear we will be gassed. Anne cries from pain, and I can't stop her from crying because I cry too. Papa may be gone. We don't know.

Every night we find more and more girls dead. One girl drooled all night, but in the morning her mouth was dry. Her hand sprawled on mine in the middle of the night. It was cold then.

She seemed peaceful. I envied her tranquility.

She had no name. But she still had her socks. I thought to take her socks. Now that she doesn't need them. But some dreadful Polish woman grabbed my arm just as I thought to pull off a sock.

Why can't I be as strong as those women!?

Anne called her an ugly cow in Dutch. The Polish woman did not care. Her feet are warm.

I don't want to see naked women anymore! I can't bear the indignity of my breasts and my privates on display. And then the guards just stand and watch as we are chosen for the chambers of gas, and I shiver from the brutal winds and I pray; I summon the Angel of Death to whisk me away, but Anne holds my hand and a part of me desists.

***

I saw baby shoes strewn on the floor when we first arrived. No one bothered to pick them up. No one needs them here.

There *are* no babies here. They killed them all a long time ago. All the orphans on our transport ran to the crematorium. They thought they arrived at a day camp. One of the guards told them that if they showered quickly they would receive lollipops before bed-time. They were all ashes by midnight.

***

I've often wondered if I would recognize the sound of peace and the silence of Palestine's night-time waters. Would the crushing waves offer Mordechai the impetus to seek refuge in my aching womb?

How I would have liked to bathe in the bliss of my husband's crushing embrace!

Instead, the fleas crush my spirit, and my misery disfigures my soul's desires.

My bed is infested. My clothes are infested. They consume my body. It no longer belongs to me. It belongs to the Nazis and the fleas. The lice and the rats.

The mud and the filth and the protruding legs and the open-mouthed skulls of the eternally shocked swim in a quagmire of death.

There are no flowers. Where are the all the butterflies?

The kind words you may hear: echoes of lullabies long past.

The walking dead join the silence of the women lying on the floor. They do not join them to bury them. They do not join them to eulogize them. They do not seek to close their eyes.

They search for the remnants of garlic or a peel of rotted beets. The pickings of the dead must go on.

We've all become scavengers here.

Some are malicious. There are thieves too. They promise you bread for your socks.

No bread. And now no socks.

If you have a gentle spirit and a soft heart the *Kapos*, the five hour roll call, the cruelties of the guards, and all this evil darkness will cause you more pain than a sea of electric shocks.

I have borne witness, and I am ready to heave my memories.

***

I need to empty my bowels, but I simply cannot bear the very thought of the latrines. Feces are everywhere. My stomach churns each time. I gag and the reflex to release is gone.

I cannot place my hands anywhere because even the walls are wet with feces. Some of the women EAT while bearing down. I have never imagined such a disgrace.

Father may be yet alive. We have no way of knowing. Mummy fears the worst, and I am beginning to doubt he is alive. The older prisoners do not live for very long. The Nazi guards find a way of disposing of the ill, or they simply expire.

Mummy fears Daddy is ill. There are rumors. We just don't know.

I have scabies too. Anne and I take turns taking care of each other. We try to keep to ourselves.

There is a lady here who wears an angora sweater. She is warm. I need her sweater if I am to live. Why can't I go back home and wear my sweaters?

Where is my Mummy? I must find her and make sure she knows I am still amongst the living.

***

She screamed, "Holland, help! Holland, help!" The Dutch lady looked oddly familiar. It was Mrs. Katz, I'm sure of it. She had typhus. They said her typhus was very severe. She was still alive, but they dumped her outside—where the dead were piled high. They use those carts—the same ones they use to empty the latrines—to empty the dead.

Holland cannot help. Pray for God to send his Angel of Death. He can help.

***

For my Mordechai:
Forgotten memory

I remember, slightly, your figure upon the hearth—
I can still recall the trembling heart,
The faltering feet—
That failed to uplift me
When I beheld you
Before me.

I can still scent the unmistakable aroma
Of unabashed fear—
I can still see the love in your eyes—
Eyes which I can no longer see.

For I have almost forgotten that which I have treasured
And promised my soul
For Eternity.
For you have disappeared and fail to return—
Leading me to despair—
And wonder—
Why are you not here?

If I can still relive the first moment we met—
Of the mutual feelings we both felt—
If I can still scent
Your being
Close to me—
Why is it that I am alone
Still waiting—
Still waiting?

Why is it that one must feel more than the other?
Why am I here—
Beginning to forget?
Surely Fire
And Passion
Which I have dreamed of
Is not another fantasy—
Waiting to become
A forgotten memory—

***

Ronnie sings for us now, and Anne and I feel a bit better when she does. She has a lovely voice, and we beg her not to stop. The scabies-barracks is a center for entertainment.

"Ronnie, sing something else! Sing the Dutch anthem!" I requested a Jewish song.

She sings songs for us all. It was lovely.

The Silent Sister

We may not stay here much longer. There are rumors the Russians are coming.

I must hide you in case the Nazis decide to transport us again.

But if I shall die or if the chambers of gas shall become my last resting stop, I pray your shit hole, your last home, will one day become fertile ground for some beautiful flowers and maybe even a majestic chestnut tree.

***

Bergen-Belsen
1945

Hell is a place here. On Earth.
    We cannot escape. The seventh gate of Ghenna—
Is here.
    For days Anne and I prayed for the train doors to open. For water. For a morsel of rotten bread or even week-old cheese. We stared at the floors—nothing but vacant stares from dead and bloated girls. And water. Just a sip. Please.
    For days I cursed the stench of urine and excrement floating in a bucket of human waste.
    Through a slit in the trains we read "Dresden", "Leipzig", "Saale", and "Salzgitter". We are in Germany. So close to my hometown. Frankfurt-am-Main.
    The wheels chugged toward the Reich, and the feces swayed back and forth and finally overturned. The remnants spilled on the corpses, and the girls used the rags of those who were long dead to soak the filth.
    Girls fell asleep and never woke up.
    The first days were filled with laments, cries, screams.
    And then silence—except for the occasional groan or gasp.
    Someone was either dying or someone discovered another corpse.
    We piled the corpses. In rows of five.
    At least this way we could lie down.
    The guards opened the cattle doors and found more dead than alive.
    The quota was met for the day.

There are no crematoria in Bergen-Belsen; they are not necessary. People die with great efficiency here.

Anne and I were separated from Mummy, and this is the cause of our overwhelming grief. We believe Daddy is no longer alive, and I fear Mummy is dead too.

I cannot bear the thought of such misery.

We lived in tents. Now we live in shacks. I hide you from prying eyes. You are my only possession. And my last secret.

There are thousands of women here. No one has a name. No one cares to ask you yours.

There is no purpose any more. Death is the life I desperately seek.

Mordechai is no longer with me. And my Mummy, my dearest, dearest Mummy may be dead too. I am an orphan. A part of me *feels* she is dead. The pit in my gut echoes, "Mummy is dead. Mummy is dead." Is she another body, dumped? Or is she a pile of ashes?

Where are you MUMMY?

***

The bodies pile up here like old books in a library.

People sleep and never awake.

They walk and collapse in mid-step.

The wind is far crueler than the absence of the sun.

I have been alone now for a long time. Anne helps me feel warm at night, and she even scavenges for food occasionally. Bread. Water!

Little does bread sustain. The soul is nearly spent. What good is some dough?

Food. We crave. Just to fill our bellies. Our empty, empty stomachs. Perhaps a morsel of rotted potato peels will only prolong our suffering? I'll give my bread to Anne today.

***

Lientje and Janny are struggling too. They are Dutch. Just like me and Anne. They sleep on a wooden bunk below ours. Anne tells us stories after we lie down. I try to regale them all, but I can never finish a story properly. Anne takes over. She knows how to tell a silly story.

We exchange silly jokes.

The Silent Sister

We compile menus in all our stories…

"Henrietta, fat and happy, goes to the American Hotel in Amsterdam for dinner and orders ham, *bolas*, and an entire cheese cake. When she is done…"

I never finished my story because Anne started to cry. She burst into tears at the thought that we would never get back to Amsterdam and eat an *entire* cheese cake.

Anne steals from the Nazis. But she never finds cheese cake. No. She finds rotten beets and a garlic peel.

***

It is Hanukkah. The festival of lights… the festival of salvation…
There is no *menorah* here. No oil. No wicks. No flames.
But there is a sliver of hope left in some of our hearts.
Janny and her sister saved scraps from their scanty bread ration. They received a special ration of Harz cheese.
So, we had a feast.
Lientje sang songs. They rewarded her with sauerkraut. The Daniels sisters and Janny and Lientje—they celebrated Christmas.
Anne said, "We are celebrating Hanukkah at the same time."
Together we sang Jewish songs. The songs Mordechai taught me at the Zionist meetings. The songs my dedicated teachers taught me at the Lyceum. The songs we learned in Maccabi Hazair. I remembered them all.
I tried to tell a story tonight, but I started to cry because Pim knows much better stories—and I thought, "He is dead."
And my Mummy I fear is long dead.

***

Dearest Mummy! My beacon. My source.
How I have never truly departed from you!
And now I sense you are no longer here on this realm called "Earth."—and I long to join you—Where can I reach you? When will I be able to see you again?
I am swimming in your waters, your warm fluid home, yet mother.

My lungs can breathe without air I am sure. For you sustain my breaths.

I dreamed a dream, and I have awakened to a nightmare.

The night is long, and daybreak far off in the distance.

Dawn no longer delights, and noon no longer inspires song.

My body shivers with a will of its own; my back aches and my head is so very hot.

I cannot feel my feet. They are frozen. I wonder if the vultures can eat frozen feet.

Anne says I have Typhus. She says we are not in Auschwitz anymore.

There is a red stain on my chest and it is not the blood from my baby's placenta.

I did dream of heat and sweat and clinging of flesh and an aching belly—but not here. In Bergen-Belsen.

Your soul, Mordechai, beseeches me far more than the even-tide's waves. The feel of your soul enveloping mine beckons me—far more than the vast ocean's expanse.

Mummy's embrace enchants me—far more than the fantasy of a blooming bud.

***

Anne's turn to take care of me. She is out hunting. We fight with our neighbors because we don't know what to do anymore. The door is always open, and we yell at everyone to close the door. Our bunk is right by the blasted doors!

The wind has blown away our house, and we don't have a warm blanket anymore. Anne says she will find some bread, but she is half-naked; I don't know if there is a supermarket in town. I think the Mediterranean desert is oasis-free, but maybe Mordechai knows a street vendor who can help us find some delicious donuts. I know of a bakery close to home, and if we're thirsty we can always drink the water from the canal. If we are really, really hungry we can grab the geese on the canal waters and break off their heads. Maybe we can start a fire. I know Mordechai knows all those tricks. He learned them in the Corps for the Advancement of the Biological systems.

Daddy always knows where to find the best beverages and chocolates in town. I should tell Anne to go to Daddy's office. Maybe we'll eat some pectin if the jam isn't ready.

I have a feeling Mummy's been calling us for some time now. She really wants us to get ready for synagogue. Hanneli promised to bring Gabriella along, and we are so excited. Maybe Mr. Goslar will let us sip the wine before the prayers because we are so thirsty tonight.

Mummy promised me a lollipop if I read Anne a book. I think Anne wants a lollipop too.

Where is my Mummy? She promised she would take us to the park, but I don't see the park.

***

It is my turn now. I welcome my Angel. I see you here. You are waiting patiently for me. How kind… Your eyes remind me of crystal waters. Your wings blow cool air unto my sweltering brow.

My body is a prison. Can you release me now? Are you from God? Is there light above, in the heavens?

My Angel's wings are white. He emits white waves of diamonds.

The world is devoid of mercy. I cannot hold on to such a world. My Angel's eyes beckon me. You seem gentle. Are you my Mummy?

The Land of the Living: not here.

This place is a factory of death.

Is your Land full of compassionate splendor?

Death is so very sweet—

Death offers vast joy and will unshackle the misery of my body's Chains upon this Earth.

Yet how saddened I am to die so soon after I was born!

For this world does linger in one's mind—

but the promises of this

Place have provided bitter fruits after all.

I have often remained long-awake trying to imagine Mordechai's body

Enveloping me with bliss.

I have envisioned my belly swelling with the evidence of my husband's love.

I have dreamed of Palestine. Jerusalem.

167

I dreamed of a world rife with wonderment and excitement. How I wished to ease a baby safely into this world, which I believed was full of beauty and charm.

I desired to hold a baby so very close to my heart. All I wanted was a family. A husband. A lover. A chance to make a difference.

But what world is this—that murders babies and kills my Mordechai?

The one man who promised me his eternal devotion?

What kind of world is this that separates a mommy from her babies?

Angel—you are silent! I look up, but I can't see. My tears blur my vision. Are you covering your face with your splendid wings? Do you have an answer? Why are you silent?

Tell me—why should I remain in a world where cruel barbarians strip you of EVERYTHING—my body is not my own, my house is gone my room is gone my school is gone my lovely Gabriella is gone my childhood is gone my innocence is destroyed and my heart bleeds even as my head aches and my palate is parched and my tears barely flow.

And now my Mummy and Daddy are dead too.

I consent to die!

Flashes of my youth spring before my eyes:

Mummy's breath. Warm milk sputters into my mouth. Papa is supporting my head. Warm words. Lullabies. Blankets. The Frankfurt countryside and bathing in the sun. I walk with mother. A kiss; a hug. The beach towel covers my knees in water so deep. Anne. A sister. A friend. A kiss for Anne.

The train ride to Holland. New home. New room.

My life whirls before me.

Prayers in synagogue. The Torah scroll rolls. Passover eve and Mrs. Goslar passes the matzo. Granny kisses me good night. And Mordechai stares at me. His eyes penetrate my soul.

The Hideaway. Bombs. Peas. Miep handing me a letter. Discovery. (This is all too fast to note!)

Westerbork. Bribing the guard. Writing in the diary in a dirty stall. Praying at night a silent prayer. The train ride of hell and the agony of what lies ahead. The torment of separation. The joy of Mordechai's pledge. The shock of his death. And the desire to join the Land of the Living.

The Silent Sister

The urgency and energy I have felt this whole night suddenly dissipates. I am now utterly depleted. And you are still waiting Angel. Silent.

My soul seeks to depart. Will you take me with you, dear Angel? Will you carry me to Mummy? Before you hold my hand… and whisk me away…

I have one final request before I bury my dearest diary in my bosom:
Come to me, sweet Mordechai, greet me
As a groom. Welcome your bride on her
Nuptials.
Mummy and Daddy lead me to my half-soul,
And baby Annalise
You can follow me to the canopy.
Greet me with song, Mordechai,
And a fiddler's soft melody.
The harmony of the heavens will sing
Our praise, and we will dance to
The sweet seraphim's eternal song.

Acknowledgements

One may ask 'How did you come up with the idea for this book?' I will be honest: I have no idea. God, I believe, paves the inspirational channels through which art manifest itself. Therefore, I must first acknowledge God and the creative, divine spirit. I pray this book illuminates the inherent beauty of the soul. I hope the spiritual light of Margot's soulfulness is aptly juxtaposed with the darkness of her time.

I must extend heartfelt appreciation to Professor Livia Bitton-Jackson for her input and generosity.

I would like to thank Mrs. Sharon Sharvit for her enthusiasm and devotion. Without any hesitation, she read and edited the manuscript, *twice*.

My dear mother for illuminating Margot's psychological struggles, especially towards the end of her short-lived life.

And of course, my dear husband for supporting all my endeavors… Thank you.

Made in the USA
Middletown, DE
27 June 2023